## As Dylan drew away, Faith tried to catch her breath.

It seemed he was doing the same. Except she wasn't sure she'd ever get her breath back again—that kiss was unlike anything she'd experienced before. In fact, if she just leaned forward a little, she could experience it again...

And then the enormity of the situation hit her.

She'd just kissed her boss.

Or he'd kissed her—she wasn't sure about the details of what had just happened. All she knew was she'd never been kissed with that much hunger. That much passion. That much mind-numbing skill. That it had been her employer, someone she shouldn't have been kissing in the first place, was a cruel twist of irony. If she'd screwed up her well-ordered plan, or caused him to not take her seriously, she'd never forgive herself.

"Faith," he said, his voice a rasp. "I'm sorry. That was completely out of line."

Honesty compelled her to point out the truth. "You weren't there alone."

\* \* \*

*Bidding on Her Boss*
is part of The Hawke Brothers trilogy:
Three tycoon bachelors, three very special mergers...

Dear Reader,

I'm so excited to share Dylan and Faith's story with you! It's the second book in The Hawke Brothers trilogy, and the third book, *His 24-Hour Wife*—about the last brother, Adam Hawke—will be out next month.

If you've read the first Hawke Brothers book, *The Nanny Proposition*, you'll have already met Dylan. At the start of that story, Jenna was working for Dylan as his housekeeper, before moving in with Liam to be nanny to Bonnie.

Dylan Hawke is the youngest Hawke brother, and he has a bit of a mischievous streak. He needed a special heroine, one who was not only as strong as he was, but who had her own dash of playfulness. Dylan thinks Faith is just that woman. Unfortunately, Faith has learned that she can only rely on herself, so Dylan has his work cut out for him convincing her otherwise. We wish him luck!

One of the lovely things about writing connected books is the chance to check in with other characters, and I relished the opportunity to have Liam, Jenna, Bonnie and Meg on the page once more. Also, knowing that I'd be seeing Dylan and Faith again when I was writing *His 24-Hour Wife* made it a little easier to say goodbye to them at the end of this book.

Thank you to all the readers who contacted me via email or social media to tell me that you enjoyed the first book in The Hawke Brothers series. I hope you enjoy this second book just as much.

Happy reading!

*Rachel*

# BIDDING
# ON HER BOSS

———

## RACHEL BAILEY

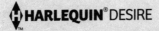

Recycling programs
for this product may
not exist in your area.

ISBN-13: 978-0-373-73412-2

Bidding on Her Boss

Copyright © 2015 by Rachel Robinson

Printed in U.S.A.

HARLEQUIN®
www.Harlequin.com

**Rachel Bailey** developed a serious book addiction at a young age (via Peter Rabbit and Jemima Puddleduck), and has never recovered. Just how she likes it. She went on to earn degrees in psychology and social work but is now living her dream—writing romance for a living.

She lives in a piece of paradise on Australia's Sunshine Coast with her hero and four dogs, where she loves to sit with a dog or two, overlooking the trees and reading books from her evergrowing to-be-read pile.

Rachel would love to hear from you and can be contacted through her website, rachelbailey.com.

### Books by Rachel Bailey

### Harlequin Desire

*Claiming His Bought Bride*
*The Blackmailed Bride's Secret Child*
*At the Billionaire's Beck and Call?*
*Million-Dollar Amnesia Scandal*
*Return of the Secret Heir*
*Countering His Claim*

### *The Hawke Brothers*

*The Nanny Proposition*
*Bidding on Her Boss*

Visit the Author Profile page at Harlequin.com or rachelbailey.com for more titles.

This book is dedicated to Sharon Archer,
who is not only an amazing author, but is also
a brilliant critique partner and very dear friend.
Sharon, thank you for being on this journey with me.

## Acknowledgments

Huge thanks to Charles Griemsman for his editing
and support with this book—Charles, it's always
a pleasure to work with you. Also, thank you to
Barbara DeLeo and Amanda Ashby
for the brainstorming and help,
and to John for always supporting my dreams.

# One

Dylan Hawke had done a few things he regretted in his life, but he had a feeling this one might top the list.

The spotlight shone in his eyes, but he smiled as he'd been instructed and gave a sweeping bow before making his way down the stairs and onto the stage. Applause—and a few cheers that he suspected were from his family—greeted him.

"We'll start the bidding at two hundred dollars," the emcee said from the front of the stage.

Dylan sucked in a breath. *And so it begins.* Step one of rehabilitating his image—donate his time to charity. Now that his brother was marrying a princess, Dylan's own mentions in the media had skyrocketed, and he'd quickly realized his playboy reputation could be a disadvantage for his future sister-in-law and the things she wanted to achieve for homeless children in LA.

"What do I hear for Dylan?" the emcee, a sitcom actor, called out. "Dylan Hawke is the man behind the chain of Hawke's Blooms florists, so we can guarantee he knows about romancing his dates."

A murmur went around the crowded room as several white paddles with black numbers shot into the air. He couldn't see too much detail past the spotlight that shone down on him, but it seemed that the place was full, and that the waiters were keeping the guests' drinks topped off as they moved through the crowd.

"Two fifty, three hundred," the emcee called.

Dylan spotted his brother Liam sitting with his fiancée, Princess Jensine of Larsland. Jenna—who had been hiding incognito as Dylan's housekeeper before she met Liam—gave him a thumbs-up. This was the first fundraising event of the new charity, the Hawke Brothers Trust, which Jenna had established to raise money for homeless children. Now that she and Liam were to be married, they planned to split their family's time between her homeland and LA, and the trust would utilize the skills she'd gained growing up in a royal family. It would be the perfect project for her—she'd said it was something she could sink her teeth into.

Dylan believed in the cause and believed in Jenna, so his job tonight was to help raise as much money as he could. He just wished he'd been able to do it in a less humiliating way. Like, say, writing a check.

But that method wouldn't help rehabilitate his image.

Which had led him to this moment. On stage in front of hundreds of people. Being sold.

"Five hundred and fifty," the emcee said, pointing at a redhead near the side of the room, whose paddle said sixty-three.

Dylan threw Sixty-Three a wink, and then crossed to where a blonde woman held up her paddle. The emcee called, "Six hundred."

Dylan squinted against the lights. There was something familiar about the blonde… Then it hit him and his gut clenched tight. It was Brittany Oliver, a local network weather girl. They'd been out two or three times a few years ago, but she'd been cloying. When he found out that she was already planning a future and children for them, he'd broken it off. He swallowed hard and sent up a prayer that someone outbid her. Maybe the cute redhead with paddle sixty-three.

He dug one hand in his pocket and flashed a charming smile at the audience—a smile he'd been using to effect since he was fourteen. He was rewarded when a stunning woman with long dark hair and coffee-colored skin raised her paddle. He was starting not to mind being on stage after all.

"Six fifty," the emcee called. "Seven hundred dollars. Seven fifty."

He knew Jenna was hoping for a big amount from this auction to get their charity started with a bang, so he took the rosebud from his buttonhole and threw it into the crowd. It was a cheesy move, but then the bidding happened so quickly that all of a sudden it hit two thousand.

Dylan steeled himself and looked over at Brittany, and sure enough, she was still in the running. He had no idea whether she'd want to chew his ear off for breaking things off or try to convince him they should get back together. Either way, it would be an uncomfortable evening. He should have had a backup plan—a signal to tell Jenna to bid whatever it took if things went awry. He could have reimbursed her later.

"Three thousand four hundred."

It was the redhead. Dylan looked her over. Bright copper hair scraped into a curly ponytail on top of her head, cobalt blue halter top, dark eyes that were wide as she watched the other bidders, and a bottom lip caught between her teeth in concentration. She looked adorable. In his pocket where the audience couldn't see, he crossed his fingers that she won. He could spend an enjoyable evening with her, a nice meal, maybe a drive to a moonlit lookout, maybe a movie.

"Four thousand six hundred."

A flash bulb went off and he smiled, but he needed to get the bidding higher for the trust. He ambled over to the emcee and indicated with a tilt of his head that he had something to say. She covered the mic with her hand and lowered it.

"Make it three dates," he said, his voice low.

Her eyebrows shot up, and then she nodded and raised the mic again. "I've just received information that the package up for auction now consists of three dates."

Over the next few minutes, there was another flurry of raised paddles before the emcee finally said, "Going once, going twice, sold for eight thousand two hundred dollars."

Dylan realized he'd stopped following the bidding and had no idea who'd won.

"Number sixty-three, you can meet Mr. Hawke at the side of the stage to make arrangements. Next we have a sports star who will need no introduction." The emcee's voice faded into the background as Dylan realized the cute redhead had made the top bid. He grinned.

Maybe turning his reputation around and doing his bit for charity wouldn't be so bad after all.

Faith Crawford stood, adjusted the hem of her halter top over her black pants and slipped between the tables to where Dylan Hawke was waiting for her by the side of the stage.

Her belly fluttered like crazy but she steeled herself and, when she reached him, stuck out her hand.

"Hi, I'm Faith," she said.

Dylan took her hand, but instead of shaking it, he lifted it to his lips and pressed a kiss on the back. "I'm Dylan, and, on behalf of my family, I appreciate your donation to the Hawke Brothers Trust."

He gave her a slow smile and her insides melted, but she tried to ignore her body's reaction. Her body didn't realize that Dylan Hawke was a notorious charmer who had probably used that exact smile on countless women. Which was why her brain was in charge. *Well*, she thought as she looked into his twinkling green eyes, *mostly in charge*.

Dylan released her hand and straightened. "I have a few ideas about places we could go on our first date—"

Faith shook her head. "I know where I want to go."

He arched an eyebrow. "Okay, then. I like a woman who knows what she wants."

Oh, she knew exactly what she wanted. And it wasn't Dylan Hawke, despite how good he looked in that tuxedo. It was what he could do for her career. She'd just made a large investment in her future—having bid most of her savings—and she wouldn't let it go to waste.

He slid a pen out of an inside pocket of his jacket and grabbed a napkin from a nearby table. "Write down your address and I'll pick you up. How does tomorrow night sound?"

The sooner the better. "Tomorrow is good. But instead of picking me up, I'd rather meet you. Let's say in front of your Santa Monica store at seven?"

He grinned, but this time it wasn't a charmer's smile. It was genuine. She liked this one more—she could imagine getting into all sorts of mischief with the man wearing that grin.

"A woman of mystery," he said, rocking back on his heels. "Nice. Okay, Faith Sixty-Three, I'll meet you in front of the Santa Monica Hawke's Blooms store at seven o'clock tomorrow night."

"I'll be there," she said and then turned and walked along the edge of the room to the door, aware that several curious gazes followed her exit. Including Dylan Hawke's. Which was just how she needed him—with his full attention focused on her.

Now all she had to do was keep her own attention soundly focused on her career, and not on getting into mischief with her date and his grin.

Dylan pulled his Porsche into the small parking lot in front of his Santa Monica store. He tried to get around to all thirty-two stores fairly regularly, but given that they were spread from San Francisco to San Diego, it didn't happen as often as it used to, and he couldn't remember exactly when he was last at this one. It looked good, though, and he knew the sales figures were in the top quarter of all the Hawke's Blooms stores.

Movement near the door caught his attention. It was Faith. Her red hair gleamed in the window lights and bounced about her shoulders. She wore a halter-neck summer dress that was fitted in all the right places and flared out over her hips, down to her knees, showing shapely calves atop stylish heels. His pulse picked up speed as he stepped out of his car.

All he knew about this woman was that she liked halter tops, her hair could stop traffic, she was wealthy enough to have spare cash lying around to help out a new charity and her lips could set his blood humming. But damn if he didn't want to know more.

"Evening, Faith," he said, walking around and opening his passenger side door.

She didn't take a step closer, just stood at the shop door looking adorable and said, "We won't be needing your car tonight."

He glanced around—the parking lot was empty. "You have a magic carpet tucked away somewhere?"

"No need," she said brightly. "We're already here."

She dug into her bag and came out with a handful of keys looped together on what looked like plaited ribbons. As he watched in surprise, she stuck a key into the front door, and he heard a click. She stepped in, efficiently disabled the alarm and turned back to him. "Come on in."

Dylan narrowed his eyes, half expecting one of his brothers to jump out and yell "gotcha" because he'd fallen for the prank. But Faith was busy putting her bag behind the counter and switching on lights. Shaking his head, he set the keyless lock on his car, followed her into the store and closed the door behind them. He had no idea what she had planned or what she really wanted out of this date, but for some reason that didn't bother him. This woman was piquing his interest on more than one level—something he hadn't experienced in a long while—and he realized he was enjoying the sensation.

"Who *are* you, Faith Sixty-Three?" he asked, leaning back against the counter and appreciating the way her dress hugged her lush curves.

She faced him then, her cheeks flushed and her warm brown eyes sparkling. "I'm a florist. My name is Faith Crawford and I work for you in this store."

Faith Crawford? That name rang a bell, but he couldn't remember any specifics. He narrowed his eyes. "Mary O'Donnell is the manager here, isn't she?"

"Yep, she's my manager," Faith said over her shoulder as she turned the light on in the storeroom in the back of the shop.

He wrapped a hand around the back of his neck. This had gone past Woman of Mystery and was fast becoming ridiculous. Why would an employee want to spend a purseful of money on a night or three with the boss? Could she have an axe to grind? Was she hoping to sleep her way to a promotion?

He blew out a breath. "How long have you worked for me?"

She turned to face him, standing a little taller. "Six months, Mr. Hawke."

"So you know Hawke's Blooms has a no fraternization policy." A policy he wholeheartedly believed in. "Managers can't be involved with anyone who works for them."

She didn't seem fazed. "I'm aware of that, yes."

"Yet," he pressed, taking a step closer and catching a whiff of her exotic perfume, "you still paid good money for a date—well, three dates—with me."

A small frown line appeared between her brows.

"Nowhere was it specified that they were supposed to be romantic *dates* with the bachelors."

Dylan was about to reply, then realized he was losing control of the conversation. "Then what do you want from me?" he asked warily.

She grabbed a clip from her handbag and pulled her hair back. "I want you to spend the evening here with me."

"Doing what, exactly?" he asked as he watched her clip her red curls, which burst out the top of the clasp in copper-colored chaos.

"Watching."

He felt his eyebrows lift. "I have to warn you, kinky propositions still fall under the no fraternization policy."

Faith rolled her eyes, but he saw the corners of her mouth twitch. "I'll be making a floral arrangement."

Right. As if he didn't get enough of that in his average day. And yet, he thought, glancing at her pale, long fingers, there was something appealing about the idea of watching Faith at work. Her fingers looked as if they'd be gentle yet firm. He could almost feel them on his jaw, then stroking across his shoulders. His skin tingled...and he realized he was getting carried away. This was not a path he could take with an employee—which he'd only just explained to her.

Besides, his attraction was probably a result of being in the store at night, alone, cocooned in the area illuminated by the lights. It couldn't be more.

He rubbed a hand down his face. "Let me get this straight. I know what you're earning, so unless you have a trust fund, your bid was a decent amount of money to you. Yet you paid it to have me sit and watch you do the job that we normally pay you to do."

She beamed at him. "That's it."

"I've missed something," he said, tilting his head to the side. She was becoming more intriguing by the minute.

She opened the fridge door and pulled out buckets of peonies, lilacs and magnolias. "Have you ever had a dream, Mr. Hawke? Something that was all yours and made you smile when you thought about it?"

Dylan frowned. His career dreams had always been for Hawke's Blooms, but they were dreams he shared with his family. Had he ever had one that was his alone?

"Sure," he said casually, knowing it was probably a lie and unsure how he felt about that.

While looking at him, she began to strip the leaves from the flower stems. "Then you know how it is."

As he took in the glow on her face, his pulse picked up speed. "What's your dream, Faith?"

She smiled mysteriously. "I have many dreams, but there's one in particular I'm trying to achieve now."

He met her gaze and the room faded away. He could have looked at her all night. Then her eyes darkened. Her breathing became irregular. Dylan wanted to groan. She felt the chemistry between them as well. His body responded to the knowledge, tightening, heating. But he couldn't let that happen. This was dangerous. He frowned and swung away.

"Tell me about the dream," he said when he turned back around, this time more in control of himself.

After a beat, Faith gave a small nod. "To open the Hawke's Blooms catalog and see one of my designs there on the page."

This was all about the catalog? He leaned back against the bench opposite the one Faith was working on and crossed his ankles. "We have a procedure in place for that."

"I know it by heart," she said, taking foam and a white tray down from the shelf. "'Any Hawke's Blooms florist may submit an original floral design to his or her manager, accompanied by a completed, signed application form. If the manager believes the design has merit, she or he will pass it to the head office to be considered for inclusion in the catalog of standard floral designs used for customer orders.'"

Dylan smiled. She'd recited the procedure word for word. "And," he added, "that process doesn't cost a single penny. Why didn't you go that route?"

"I did." She clipped the bottoms from a bunch of peony stems. "About twenty times, in fact. After my manager rejected number sixteen, I began to think that way might not work for me." She smiled and her dimples showed.

He thought about her manager, Mary O'Donnell. Mary was simpering to management, which was annoying, but he knew she ran a tight ship. Was it possible she was blocking her own staff from advancement? "Are you making a complaint about your manager?" he asked, serious.

She shook her head, and her hands slowed to a stop as she met his gaze. "I'm a good florist, Mr. Hawke. I take pride in my work, and take direction from my manager. I do my best by our customers and have a good group of regulars who ask for me by name. So I don't think it's too much to ask to have just one of my designs considered so I can move my career forward."

Dylan knew he was lucky—he'd grown up in the family business, where his input had been not only lis-

tened to but also encouraged. But what if he'd been in
Faith's shoes? An employee of a large company who
was struggling to have her voice heard. He watched her
place flowers in the foam, turning the arrangement with
the other hand as she went. He'd like to think he'd have
gone the extra mile, the way Faith was doing tonight.

"So you decided to get creative," he said, hearing the
trace of admiration in his own voice.

"Seeing you were auctioning off a night of your time
seemed like a sign." She glanced up at him, her long-
lashed eyes earnest. "Do you believe in destiny, Mr.
Hawke?"

"Can't say it's something I've ever paid much attention to," he said. Unlike, say, the way the side of her
jaw sloped down to her neck, or the sprinkling of pale
ginger freckles across her nose.

"Well, I do, and I'd just been thinking 'If only I could
speak to someone in the head office myself' when the
posters for the auction went up in the window. The
very window where I work." She paused, moistening
her lips. "You can see it was too strong a sign to ignore, can't you?"

He wasn't sure if he wanted to chuckle or to kiss
those full lips her tongue had darted over. Instead, he
murmured, "I suppose so."

"So I attended the auction, used a good portion of my
savings, and here we are." She splayed her free hand to
emphasize her point, and then picked up a roll of ribbon
and went back to what she was doing.

Dylan shifted his weight. Something about this
situation and her confidence was beginning to make
him uncomfortable. After she'd spent that amount of
money—which he'd reimburse now that he knew she

was an employee trying to get a meeting with him—
and she'd gone to this much effort, how would she react
if he agreed with her manager?

"Tell me, Faith," he said carefully. "What happens
if, after all this effort and expense, I don't like your design enough to put it in the catalog?"

She looked him in the eye again. There was no arti-
fice, no game playing in her deep brown gaze. "Then
I'll know I've given it my best shot, and I'll work harder
to create an even better design."

Dylan nodded. She believed in herself but didn't have
a sense of entitlement and was prepared to put in the
work to improve her situation. He liked her attitude.
In fact, there were a number of things he liked about
Faith Crawford—including things he shouldn't allow
himself to like now that he knew she worked for him.
Such as the crazy hair that his fingers were itching to
explore, and the way her sweet-shaped mouth moved
as she spoke.

There was also a vibrancy about her that dragged
his gaze back every time he looked away. How would
it feel to hold all that vibrancy in his arms? Her kisses
would be filled with passion, he just knew it, and in his
bed… Dylan held back a groan and determinedly refo-
cused on Faith's floristry skills.

Her movements were quick and economical but still
flowed, almost as if her hands were dancing. He'd had a
stab at displaying flowers in the past but hadn't pulled
off more than rudimentary arrangements. It had been
enough for the roadside stall his family had started the
business with but hadn't come close to what a florist
with training and flair could create. Yet having been

around professional florists for his entire adult life, he was good at spotting skill in someone else.

He could already tell that Faith didn't just have the training all florists employed by Hawke's Blooms stores required. She also had that indefinable, creative *something* that differentiated the great from the good. Whether she'd harnessed that talent, and was able to use it to create designs of the standard needed to be included in the catalog, was yet to be seen.

But if nothing else, tonight Faith Crawford had achieved one thing she'd set out to achieve—she definitely had his full attention.

In fact, he was having trouble looking anywhere but at her.

Faith added another peony to the arrangement and tried to ignore the prickles on the back of her neck that told her Dylan was watching her again. Of course, that's what the whole night had been engineered to achieve, but he was only sometimes following what her hands were doing. At other times...

Heat rose in her belly as she thought about the way he'd been staring at her mouth a few minutes ago. She couldn't remember the last time a man had looked at her with that much hunger. Especially a man she'd been wanting to wrap herself around and kiss as if there was no tomorrow ever since he'd stepped out of his sex-on-wheels car.

And that it had to be Dylan Hawke, the CEO of the company? Well, that was fate playing a cruel joke on her. So she pretended that she wasn't wildly attracted to the man in front of her and that he wasn't sending her the same signals. She focused on the flowers. Which was working out fairly well, except for the prickles on the back of her neck.

But she needed to concentrate, to stop letting herself be distracted. Ruthlessly she reminded herself of what was at stake: getting this right could mean a fantastic boost to her career. She turned the arrangement with quick flicks of her wrist, checking for symmetry. Just a few stray leaves to trim. She snipped them away carefully. It looked good, balanced in color and form... but was it special enough to go into the catalog? She'd controlled her wilder artistic urges and gone for a safer conservative arrangement to impress. Butterflies fluttered mercilessly in her stomach. For the first time, she realized how much Mary's criticism had dented her confidence in her creativity.

She reached out to touch a crisp green leaf. This arrangement was finished—but still she hesitated.

"All done?"

She jolted at the sound of Dylan's voice so close to her ear. Last time she'd been aware of him, he'd been on the other side of the bench. She tried to move to the side. Her foot caught on something and she felt herself begin to fall. A hand closed around her arm, and her almost certain tumble was averted. She closed her eyes, and then opened them to find Dylan staring at her. The picture of him on the company website was nothing like the living, breathing man before her.

With him so close, no more than a hand span away, his scent surrounded her. It was dark and mysterious, surprising. She'd have expected something lighter, more recognizable, perhaps one of the expensive name-brand colognes. Yet this had undertones of a night in the forest—earthy, secretive and alluring. A shiver ran down her body to her toes. Dylan stilled.

Her breath caught in her throat. She could feel the heat from his body reaching out to envelop her. The world receded around her and all she could see, all she could feel, was Dylan. His eyes darkened and she swallowed hard. She should step away, not let her body lead her into temptation. But, oh, what temptation this man was. She could feel her pulse thundering at the base of her throat and saw Dylan's gaze drop to observe the same thing.

"Faith," he murmured, his breathing uneven.

She closed her eyes, fighting the effect of hearing her name on his lips, and when she opened them again, he was closer than before, his breath fanning over her face. Her hands found their way to his chest, so solid and warm.

A shudder ran down his body at her touch.

"Please—" she said, and before she could finish the thought his mouth was on hers. A small part of her mind told her to pull away, but instead, her hands fisted in his shirt, not letting him go.

He groaned as she opened her mouth to him, and his arms wrapped around her, holding her close while pushing her back against the workbench. His tongue was like nothing else as it stroked along the side of hers, leaving her wanting more. To be closer. So much closer.

She was lost.

# Two

As Dylan drew away, Faith tried to catch her breath. It seemed as if he was doing the same. Except she wasn't sure she'd ever get her breath back again—that kiss was unlike anything she'd experienced before. In fact, if she just leaned forward a little, she could experience it again…

And then the enormity of the situation hit her, sending her knees wobbling.

She'd just kissed her boss.

No, not *her* boss—the *big* boss. She'd just kissed the man with ultimate responsibility for every single Hawke's Blooms store.

Or he'd kissed her—she wasn't sure about the details of what had just happened. All she knew was she'd never been kissed with that much hunger. That much passion. That much mind-numbing skill. That it had been her employer, someone she shouldn't have been kissing in the first place, was a cruel twist of irony. If she'd screwed up her well-ordered plan or caused him to not take her seriously, she'd never forgive herself.

"Faith," he said, his voice a rasp. "I'm sorry. That was completely out of line."

Honesty compelled her to point out the truth. "You weren't there alone."

"But I'm the one who's the boss." He winced. "It's my responsibility not to cross the damn line. You shouldn't feel pressured or uncomfortable in your workplace, and I apologize."

"I don't feel uncomfortable. Well," she amended, looking down at her hands, "I didn't feel uncomfortable or pressured *then*. I guess I'm uncomfortable now." She glanced back up, meeting his wary gaze. "But you should know, I wanted to kiss you. Then."

His head tilted to the side. "But not now?"

"No." Which was a lie. She definitely wanted to kiss him again. Wanted it more than almost anything. The key was the *almost*. She wanted a flourishing career more than she wanted to kiss Dylan Hawke again.

He blew out a breath. "That's a relief, but it's not enough. It was selfish of me to kiss you when you wanted me here for a completely different purpose. I give you my word it won't happen again."

"I appreciate that," she said, trying to conjure a professional facade.

He was silent for a couple of beats, his gaze assessing. "You seem quite certain, considering you just said you'd wanted me to kiss you only a few minutes ago."

She wasn't sure where he was coming from—it didn't look like flirting, but she couldn't read him well enough to know. Maybe he was testing her, wanting to ensure she wasn't going to change her mind and make waves in the company. Whatever it was about, she had to be absolutely clear so he understood her position.

She drew in a breath and lifted her chin. "Boyfriends and lovers aren't hard to come by, Mr. Hawke. What I need more than a man is someone to appreciate my talent. I hope this isn't offensive, but I want you professionally more than personally."

He flashed her a self-deprecating smile. "Understood. Which means I'd better have a look at this arrangement."

She stood back to give him some room. Everything she'd done recently, from making the plan to attending the auction to spending most of her savings to meeting Dylan here tonight, had led to this moment. It was the do-or-die moment, and all she could do was step back, cross her fingers and hope he'd still give an honest assessment after he'd kissed her.

Dylan dug his hands in his pockets as he faced her arrangement. He moved around, looking at it from several angles before straightening with a grimace.

"That bad?" she asked, her stomach in free fall. "You're grimacing."

"No, it's not bad." He leaned back against the bench and crossed his arms over his chest. "If I'm not smiling it's because I really wanted to put your arrangement in the catalog."

She felt the words like a slap. Tears pressed against the backs of her eyes, but she wouldn't let them form. "But you're not going to."

"I'm sorry, Faith," he said, his voice gentle. "Especially after…" He gestured toward the other end of the bench, where they'd been when he'd kissed her.

She bit down on her lip. She might feel bad, but she didn't want him to feel bad as well. He was only doing his job. "Don't apologize. If it's not good enough, that's my problem, not yours."

"The thing is, it's good, really good, but it looks a lot like the arrangements that are already in the book. If we add something new, then it needs to be unique. It has to offer our customers a genuine alternative to the options already there, and this arrangement, though beautiful, is—"

"Too much like what they can already choose," she finished for him, understanding his point, but still deflated.

He moved closer and laid a hand on her shoulder, his eyes kind. "But I'll reimburse the money you paid at the auction. You shouldn't have to pay to have an appointment with someone at the head office."

Her back stiffened. He wasn't going to wriggle out of this that easily. "I won't take the money back. I have two more *dates* left and I plan to use them."

There was no way she was giving up this direct line to the head of the Hawke's Blooms stores. It had been a good plan when she'd made it, and it was still a good plan…as long as she hadn't blown her chances by kissing him.

Sure, tonight hadn't been the raging success she'd hoped for, but there were two more dates yet. When she set her mind to something, she didn't give up until she'd achieved it. She'd impress him yet and get one of her arrangements in the catalog.

He dropped his hand and sighed. "The thing is, Faith,

I can't force you to take the money back, but it would be easier for me if you did."

"Perhaps," she said and smiled sweetly. "But it wouldn't be easier for me."

"Look, can I be honest?"

He thrust the fingers of both hands through his hair and left them there, linking them behind his head. This wasn't the same man who'd kissed her moments before, or the man who ran an entire chain of retail stores, or even the man who'd confidently strutted the stage at the auction. This one seemed more real.

She nodded. "Please."

"I'm in the process of trying to rehabilitate my image." He gave her half a smile, and she tried not to laugh at how adorable he looked now.

"From playboy to the future brother-in-law of a princess?"

He shifted his weight to his other leg. "Yeah, something like that."

"So to stop people seeing you as a playboy, you auctioned yourself off to the highest bidder?" She jumped up to sit on the bench, enjoying his discomfort more than she would have expected, but also enjoying seeing this private side of him.

He coughed out a laugh. "Yeah, when you put it like that, it sounds crazy."

Suddenly she was more than intrigued. This man was a mass of contradictions and she wanted to know more. To understand him. "Then how would you put it?"

"I'm throwing myself into our new charity. The auction was only the first step, but I'll be involved every step of the way."

"A respectable, upstanding member of the community." She could see him pulling it off, too. Going from a playboy to a pillar of the community.

"So you can see that the very last thing I need is a scandal involving a staff member, especially given that we have a policy about management being involved with staff."

A scandal? She frowned. What, exactly, did he think she wanted from those other two dates? "Dylan, I'm not expecting romance on the other dates any more than I expected it on this one."

He shrugged one shoulder. "But image is everything."

That was true. She cast her mind around for a solution. There was no way she was giving up her remaining dates without a fight. "What if no one knows? We could do them in secret."

"That boat pretty much sailed when the auction was covered by the media," he said and chuckled. Then he sobered and let out a long breath. "But it's more than that."

Understanding dawned. "Our kiss changed things." She said the words softly, as if acknowledging the truth too loudly would make a difference.

He nodded, his gaze not wavering from her eyes. "And it's very important that I see you only as an employee, and you see me only as a boss."

"I won't have any trouble with that. Are you saying you will?" She arched her eyebrow in challenge, guessing Dylan Hawke was a man who didn't shrink from a challenge.

One corner of his mouth kicked up. "If you can do it, I can."

"Then it looks like we don't have a problem, do we?"

Knowing he was trapped in the logic of it, she jumped down from the bench and grabbed the trash.

She felt him behind her, not moving, probably assessing his options. Then finally he took the trash can from her and began to sweep stem cuttings together with his free hand.

"It appears you've won this round, Faith Sixty-Three," he said from beside her.

She flashed him a wry smile. "Dylan, if I'd won this round, my design would soon be featured in the catalog. All I've done is kept the door open for another round."

"You know what?" he said, his voice amused. "Even though I know I shouldn't be, I'm already looking forward to the next round."

She turned and caught his gaze, finding a potent mix of humor and heat there—something closer to the real man she'd glimpsed earlier. Quickly she turned away. This was going to be hard enough without seeing him as anything more than the head of the Hawke's Blooms stores. And she had a sinking feeling it might already be too late for that anyway…

Two days later, Dylan pulled into the parking lot of the Santa Monica store. He hadn't done an all-day inspection for a while. It used to be part of his management style—show up in the morning unannounced, hang around in the background and help out where he could. Nothing beat it for getting a good feel for how a store was working and what needed improvement.

He'd been meaning to start doing a couple of these a month, so his office staff hadn't thought there was anything strange when he'd told them to clear his schedule for today. Of course, they weren't to know what he was

trying to deny to himself—that he hadn't stopped thinking about one of the Santa Monica store's employees
since the moment he'd dropped her home that first night.

Under different circumstances, there was no question
he'd ask her out. That kiss had been beyond amazing
and had been on an automatic replay loop in his mind
ever since, but he'd also enjoyed her company. He never
knew what she was going to say or do next, and that
made her fun to be around.

He sighed and stepped from his car. No use wasting
energy wanting what he couldn't have. She worked for
him. End of story.

But that didn't stop him from wondering how this
particular store was doing. Despite rejecting Faith's arrangement himself, he'd been left wondering if her manager was doing all she could for the advancement of her
staff if Faith had put in twenty applications to the catalog of standard arrangements and not one had made it
through to the head office.

Sure, he'd rejected the one he'd seen last night, but
given Faith's enthusiasm and skill, a good, supportive
manager should have found a way to guide her toward
a more appropriate arrangement by now. Perhaps even
submitted one or two just to encourage her. Yes, it was
definitely time he had a closer look at how this store—
and the other stores—were doing.

As he stepped through the front door and removed
his aviator sunglasses, the manager, Mary O'Donnell,
looked up and waved enthusiastically.

"Mr. Hawke!" she called, her voice obsequious. "So
good to see you. Here, Faith, take over this arrangement.
I need to talk to Mr. Hawke."

At the mention of his name, Faith froze, then looked

up like a deer caught in headlights. Her tongue darted out to moisten her lips, and he was assailed by memories of her mouth. Of how incredible it had felt under his. Of how it had opened to allow his tongue entry. Before he could forget all the reasons not to kiss her again, he determinedly drew his gaze to Mary O'Donnell.

"No need," he said. "I'm here for the day. Don't stop what you're doing—I just want to get a feel for the store."

"You haven't done an all-day inspection for quite a while." Mary shot a suspicious glance around the room. "Is there a problem?"

"Just continuing a procedure that worked well for us in the past. I've let it slip a bit as we've grown, but I'll be working my way around to all the stores in the coming months."

"And we're first?" she asked, pride beaming from her features.

"Yes, you are." He'd let her think it was a compliment. Plus, it was a much more professional reason than the fact that he hadn't been able to stop thinking about one of her employees.

"Well, in that case, let me introduce you to the team." She grabbed a middle-aged blonde woman by the wrist and dragged her over. "This is Courtney. She's our senior florist. If you want any bouquets made to take home at the end of the day, Courtney's your woman."

"Good to meet you, Courtney," he said, shaking her hand.

Courtney smiled openly. "Nice to meet you, too, Mr. Hawke. Though, if you don't mind, I need to finish this order before the courier arrives in a few minutes?"

"Of course," he said and watched her go back to

work on one of the long benches. She seemed efficient and nice enough, and the arrangement she was working on was good.

"And this is our other florist, Faith Crawford," the manager said, pointing in Faith's direction. He watched the reactions of the other two women closely, checking to see if they knew Faith was the person who'd won the bid at the auction, but neither gave anything away. Interesting. Faith obviously hadn't told them, and the company grapevine hadn't caught up with the news yet. Most of the staff from the head office had been at the auction the other night, but even if they'd managed to get a good look at Faith in the dim light, it seemed none had recognized her.

He glanced over at her now. She had a bright yellow Hawke's Blooms apron covering the halter top he could see peeking out from underneath. Her curly red hair was caught up in a clip on the top of her head. She looked up and he paused, waiting to see her reaction. Her eyes flicked to her manager, then back to him. He wasn't comfortable with an outright lie to his employees—it was probable that the information would circulate around the company at some point, and he didn't want to be caught in a lie—but that didn't mean he had to share all the details of their short history.

"Ms. Crawford and I have met before," he said as a compromise.

The manager's eyes darted between them, looking for snippets of information, so he cut her off at the pass. "Do you have an apprentice in this store?"

"Oh, yes. Sharon. But she's not in until lunchtime on Mondays."

He nodded and took off his sport coat. Instead of his

usual work attire of a business suit, today he'd worn a polo shirt and casual trousers—closer to the clothes the staff in-store wore. "Before she gets here, I'll do the sweeping and answering the phone. Wherever you need an extra pair of hands."

Unbidden, his gaze tracked to where Faith worked at her bench, and he found that she'd looked up at him at the same time. *Wherever you need an extra pair of hands*... He could still feel his hands in her hair, cupping her cheek, under her chin.

A pink flush crept up Faith's neck to her cheeks, and he knew she was remembering the same thing. He cleared his throat and looked away.

If he was going to make it through the day without letting everyone know he'd kissed his employee, he would have to do better at keeping his thoughts firmly under control.

It had been two hours since Dylan had appeared in the doorway, looking as if he'd just stepped off a photo shoot for a story entitled "What the Suave CEOs Are Wearing This Season." She'd spent those two hours trying to pretend he wasn't in the room, just so she could get her work done.

But every time he swept up the clippings from where she was working, or he handed her a slip of paper with an order that had come in over the phone, she lost the battle and was plunged back into those moments when they'd been in this very spot, at night, alone.

And occasionally, when their eyes met, she thought she saw the same memory lurking in his.

But she couldn't let herself be sidetracked. She needed to impress the businessman, Mr. Hawke, not the red-blooded Dylan who'd kissed her senseless. Men came and went, but this particular man could help her career. It was Mr. Hawke she needed to impress with what she could do.

They'd had a steady stream of orders in person, over the phone and on their website, and she was glad. It gave her an excuse not to talk to Dylan—no, Mr. Hawke—just yet. He'd sat with Courtney earlier and had a cup of coffee, asking her about her job and ideas for the store, and said he'd be doing the same with all the staff members.

The bell above the door dinged, and she looked up, smiling to see one of her favorite customers.

"Hi, Tom," she said, heading for the fridge. "How was your weekend?"

"Not long enough," he said ruefully. "Yours?"

Her eyes flicked to Dylan, who was thumbing through their order book, his dark reddish-brown hair rumpled, his sport coat gone and his tie loosened. His hand hesitated and his chest expanded as if he'd taken a deep breath.

"How about I go with *interesting*," she said, turning back to her customer.

Tom laughed. "Sounds as if there's a story there."

"My life is never dull." She reached into the fridge and drew out the assorted foliage she'd put to the side earlier. "I found some fresh mint at the markets this morning, as well as these cute little branches of crab apples. How does that sound?"

"Like a winner. Emmie loved the daisy and rosemary bouquet last week."

Out of the corner of her eye, she saw Dylan watching the conversation and then moving to her elbow. He put his hand out to Tom. "Hi, I'm Dylan Hawke, CEO of the Hawke's Blooms retail chain."

"Wow, the big boss," Tom said, winking at Faith.

Dylan turned to her. "You bought crab apples and mint yourself for this bouquet?" His tone was mild, but his focus had narrowed in on her like a laser pointer. "This sounds interesting. Can you talk me through the thinking behind your plan?"

Her stomach clenched tight. She'd wanted the attention of the businessman side of him, and now she had it, which was great. But if he thought what she was doing was too bizarre, then she might have lost her chance to win his approval. A second strike against her in a row might be too much to overcome.

All she could do was paste on a smile and do her job.

"Tom comes in each Monday to pick up some flowers for his wife," she said, her gaze on the work her hands were doing. "Emmie is blind, so I always put some thought into combinations that she can enjoy."

"You picked up the mint on your way in?" Dylan asked, his tone not giving anything away.

She nodded. "Monday mornings I leave home a bit earlier and drop in at the flower markets, looking for some inspiration. We usually go outside the standard range of flowers that the store stocks to get the right elements for Emmie's bouquet. I like something fragrant—" she picked up the mint "—and something tactile—" she pointed to the crab apple branch "—along with the usual assortment of flowers."

She cast a glance at the buckets bursting with bright blooms around them, looking for inspiration. *Something white, perhaps?*

Dylan raised an eyebrow and she hesitated. Maybe

he didn't like florists going this far off the beaten track? Her manager hadn't been particularly supportive and always complained if she tried to get reimbursement for the extras from petty cash, but Faith loved the challenge of something new each week, and the fact that Tom wanted to do this for his wife always melted her heart. Were there other men like Tom in the world? Men who were so dedicated to bringing a smile to the faces of the women they loved that they'd go the extra mile every single week? That sort of constancy was a beautiful thing to be a part of.

Perhaps Dylan Hawke didn't see the situation the same way. She held a sprig of mint out to him. "If that's okay, Mr. Hawke?"

"More than okay," he said, taking the mint and lifting it to his nose. "I think it's a great example of customer service."

Dylan's approving gaze rested on her, and her shoulders relaxed as relief flowed through her veins. But she was also aware that his approval was having more of an effect than it should...

As she worked, he blended into the background, but she felt his eyes on her the entire time she was making the crab apple, mint and white carnation arrangement. After Tom left, pleased with the results, Dylan cornered her near the cash register.

"Please tell me you get reimbursed for those extras you purchase on Monday mornings," he said, his voice low.

She maintained a poker face. Getting her manager into trouble was a quick route to reduced hours, but she couldn't lie, either. He could check the store's accounting books and find that she hadn't asked for reimbursement after the first few times, not since Mary had finally put her foot down and said she should use stock that was already in the store. And being caught in a lie by the CEO would be even less healthy for her career than not covering for her immediate manager.

"Sure, but sometimes I forget to hand the receipts in," she said in what she hoped was a casual, believable tone.

"I see," he said, and she had a feeling he really did see.

"I don't mind paying for those extras," she said quickly. "I know I should only use what we have in stock, but I get such a kick out of Tom's expression when he knows he's taking home something Emmie will love. It's like a present I can give them."

"It's your job, Faith. You shouldn't have to pay money to do your job." He crossed his arms over his chest. "Do you have the receipt from this morning?"

She picked up her handbag from under the counter and dug around until she found the crumpled bit of paper. "Here," she said, passing it to him.

Their hands brushed, and she couldn't help the slight gasp that escaped at the contact. Tingles radiated from the place they'd touched, and she yearned to reach out and touch him again. On his hand, or his forearm. Or— she looked up to his face—the cheek she'd stroked with her fingertips when they'd kissed. His eyes darkened.

"Faith," he said, his voice a rasp, "we can't."

"I know," she whispered.

"Then don't—"

"Anything I can help you with, Mr. Hawke?" Mary asked from behind them.

Without missing a beat, Dylan turned, his charming

smile firmly in place, where only seconds before she'd seen something real, something raw.

"I was just chastising your florist about not submitting her receipts for the extras she's been buying for that customer's weekly order." He handed over the receipt. "Ms. Crawford has promised she'll turn them in to you from now on, haven't you, Ms. Crawford?"

"Ah, yes," Faith said, not meeting her manager's eyes. "If you'll excuse me, I have another order to make up."

She slipped away and left them to their discussion, finally able to take a full breath again only when she was immersed in her next arrangement. This day couldn't end soon enough. He was too close here. In her space. Making her want him.

Yet even if he weren't the owner of the company, the last man she could give her heart to was a man whose love life had no stability. She'd heard the rumors about Dylan, that he changed female companions regularly, never seeming to form attachments. She couldn't fall for someone like that—she wouldn't do it to herself. She'd spend the entire time waiting for the moment he'd move on. Better to stay independent and create stability by relying on herself.

She repeated the words to herself over and over while she worked, the whole time trying to ignore her body's awareness of where he was in the room. And resisting the urge to walk over and touch him again.

# Three

By late afternoon, Dylan was back in his office, staring out the window at the LA skyline. He had achieved what he'd set out to that morning—a detailed understanding of how the Santa Monica store was operating. He'd managed to sit down with all four employees during the day and chat about their perceptions and ideas, and had seen for himself that the customers were pleased with the floral arrangements being produced.

He'd also discovered one other thing—this fledgling attraction for Faith Crawford wasn't going to fade away. From the moment he arrived, he'd fought to stop his gaze traveling to her. Wherever she was in the store, he could feel her. And occasionally he'd caught her watching him with more than an employee's interest. His heart picked up speed now just thinking about it.

He'd cursed the Fates that he'd had to meet her while she worked for him.

He'd also noticed she was far from an average employee. He'd been taking orders over the phone and in person all day from people who wanted only an arrangement made by Faith. When he'd tried to suggest that another florist serve them, they'd said they'd wait. And he could see why. Her arrangements were spectacular. Why had she made such a conservative design the night she'd tried to impress him? When she was in her element, her work was original and beautiful. They were designs he wanted in the catalog so florists in the other stores were reproducing them.

And the bouquet she'd made using mint and crab apples for the man to give his blind wife had been the most cutting-edge design Dylan had seen in a long time. He liked it when staff went the extra mile for customers, adding that personal touch, and her customers seemed to appreciate it. In fact, just about everything about Faith impressed him. On every level, from the professional to the personal to the physical...

His skin heated.

Shaking his head, he focused back on the professional.

Faith Crawford was someone with a lot of potential. And he wanted to help her reach that potential for the benefit of Hawke's Blooms, and because he really wanted to see Faith get her just rewards. That manager of hers wasn't going to recognize her talents anytime soon, despite the overwhelming evidence under her nose.

He grabbed the phone on his desk and dialed Human Resources. "Anne, do you have a minute?" he asked when the head of HR picked up.

"Sure. What do you need, Dylan?"

"I did an impromptu inspection at the Santa Monica store today."

"Great," she said brightly. "You always bring back good feedback when you do one of those. What do you have for me?"

He dug one hand in his trouser pocket and looked out over the skyline. "One of the florists there has a lot of potential, and I want to do something about that."

"What was her name?"

"Faith Crawford," he said, ensuring his voice was even and didn't give away his reaction to her.

There was a pause, and he could hear fingers tapping on a keyboard as Anne brought up Faith's file. "What do you have in mind?"

"Her work is good. Really good. Original and creative. But in the interest of full disclosure, I should let you know that Faith is the person who bought the dates with me at the trust's bachelor auction."

"I was sorry to miss that night, it sounded like a lot of fun," Anne said, chuckling. "So how do you want to handle this from here?"

He rubbed a hand through his hair. "She's got a lot of potential, and I want to see Hawke's Blooms benefit from that, but I don't want any suggestion that she bought her way into a promotion. How about you get someone else to go out and assess her? Don't tell them that the idea came from me, just let them go to the Santa Monica store without any preconceptions and see her work."

"I'll see what I can arrange and let you know."

"Thanks, Anne."

He hung up the phone, feeling very satisfied with his day's work. The only thing that could make it better was to be the one who actually gave Faith the promotion, so he could be there when she found out about it. But he didn't want her to think this had anything to do with their kiss, so it was better that she had a fair and independent assessment first. He had no doubt that whoever did that would see what he'd seen and recommend her for something more senior.

But still, a good day's work indeed. He smiled, thinking about Faith's reaction. She was going to be over the moon.

As Faith picked out a long-stemmed apricot rose from the bucket at her feet, Mary appeared across the bench from her with a folded piece of paper in her hand.

"I've just had a call from head office about you," she said, her voice accusing.

Faith stopped what she was doing and looked up. "About me personally?"

Besides the initial paperwork when she'd started at the store, she hadn't had any direct dealings with the head office other than the impersonal pay slips. She wiped her hands on her apron and waited.

Mary planted her hands on her hips. "Have you been talking to the head office without my knowledge?"

"Of course not," Faith said, and then realized she'd been talking to Dylan on the weekend without her manager knowing. And would be talking to him again about their next two dates. But he had her phone number—he wouldn't be contacting her via her manager.

Hands still on her hips, Mary lifted her chin as she spoke. "It was Anne in Human Resources. They're offering you a promotion."

Faith's breath caught. *Hang on...*

"A promotion?" she repeated, trying to make sense of it.

"To the head office." Mary thrust the piece of paper at her. "They emailed the details."

Faith took the paper but didn't want to open it in front of the entire store. "I'll be back in a few minutes," she said and went out the back door to the lane. Then she opened the folded email printout.

It was a formal letter of promotion to the head office. To a desk job. She scanned the list of duties and found they were all things that didn't involve customers. Or flowers.

Frustration started simmering in her belly. She'd spent most of her life being told what would happen to her. Announcements would come that she'd be moving to another family member's house the next week, that she'd have to change schools, that her father would be visiting and taking her to a theme park, that he would be returning her to yet another relative afterward. The best thing about being an adult was that she was in charge of her own life.

So getting notice out of the blue saying she was being moved to a desk job that she hadn't applied for and certainly didn't want was particularly unwelcome.

She was ambitious, yes, but not for just any promotion. She had a very clear vision of what she wanted in her career, and this job—being stuck in a boring office, away from customers and the daily joy of working with flowers—wasn't it.

Besides, was this really out of the blue?

She'd kissed the CEO, and in less than a week he'd come to the store for a full-day inspection—something the others said he used to do, but hadn't done since she'd been working there. And now a promotion.

What was Dylan Hawke really up to?

The thought made her uneasy, so she went back through the door and told Mary that she was declining the offer.

Dylan drove into the parking lot of the Santa Monica store for the third time in a week, still not sure what to make of the call he'd had from Anne telling him Faith had turned down the promotion. With all her ambition, he'd expected her to leap at the opportunity. So, surprised and intrigued, he'd jumped into his car to talk to her face-to-face.

As he walked through the door, Mary dropped what she was doing and headed for him, her face covered in a fawning smile. Faith wasn't in sight, and he was more disappointed than he should have been at not seeing an employee.

Then she walked in from the cold room, carrying a bucket full of flowers. She was wearing black biker boots that almost reached her knees and a bright purple dress that peeked out around the yellow Hawke's Blooms apron. Her wild hair was caught up on top of her head and sprang out in all directions. He only barely resisted a smile—this woman was a force of nature.

Her step faltered when she saw him.

"Mr. Hawke!" Mary said when she reached him, darting suspicious glances at Faith. "Twice in one week. We're honored."

He paused before answering. He hadn't planned what he should say here—how had the offer of the promotion gone down at the store level? Should he mention it now, or play it cool for the moment? He glanced across at her as she pulled stems one by one from the bucket. His gut was telling him not to mention it until he'd at least spoken to Faith.

He smiled at Mary. "I just have a few follow-up questions from the other day."

"Well, I'm at your service," she said, untying the apron strings at her back. "Would you like to talk here, or perhaps at the café next door?"

"Actually, I'd like to talk to Faith if she has a few minutes."

Faith's hands stilled and her face grew pale. He was torn between wanting to reassure her and wanting to demand an explanation. Instead, he turned an expectant expression to Mary.

"Of course, Mr. Hawke. If that's what you want." But her face was sour. She really didn't like Faith getting more attention than her.

"Excellent." He smiled and rocked back on his heels. "You mentioned a café next door?"

Mary's mouth opened and closed again. "Er, yes. Courtney can finish that order. Faith. Can you come and talk to Mr. Hawke, please?"

"Certainly," Faith said, wiping her hands on her apron and removing it. The entire time, she kept her gaze down.

"Thank you," he said to Mary, and then opened the door for Faith and followed her out onto the pavement.

"Have I just made things difficult for you in there?" he asked.

She lifted her chin. "Nothing I can't deal with."

He was beginning to see how true that was. Faith Crawford was most definitely her own woman. From bidding on the CEO of her company at a charity auction to get his attention for her work, to turning down a promotion most of his staff would jump at and not bowing to the head office... The more he got to know this woman, the more he liked her.

They found a secluded booth at the café and ordered coffees.

"I heard you were offered a promotion." He leaned back and rested his arm along the top of the padded vinyl booth. "You turned it down."

The corners of her mouth twitched. "You *heard* I was offered the job? Are you sure you don't mean you *arranged* for me to be offered the job?"

He grinned. The fact that she spoke her mind was a very attractive feature. "Okay, I might have had a hand in it. After watching you in the store for a day, I realized your potential was being underutilized, and I implemented a plan to rectify that."

"Is that all it was?" She arched an eyebrow and waited.

"You think it's about more?" His gaze dropped to her mouth, and his pulse picked up speed. "You think you were being promoted because I'd kissed you?"

"Maybe it wasn't that straightforward, but we kissed, and suddenly the store has an all-day inspection and I get offered a job in the head office. Tell me that's not a coincidence." Her gaze didn't waver, challenging him to be honest.

"It's not a coincidence, but it's not direct cause and effect, either—there were steps in between. When you talked about your store and your designs not being submitted for the catalog, it made me wonder what was going on here, and I came to check it out. That's when I realized your potential."

She tapped her nails on the table, but the rest of her barely moved. "So it wasn't payback of some kind? Or a way to assuage your guilt about kissing an employee?"

"I don't work that way." He tried not to be insulted, given that she didn't know him very well, but it was good at least to have her concerns addressed now, before they had their other two dates. "I passed your name to HR with a suggestion that they check you out. They arranged a couple of people to come in as customers and ask for you so they could see your skills and how you interact with customers, and then one of the staff from the head office dropped in to see Mary and watched you while she was there. Her name was Alison—she chatted to you for a while on your break, apparently. You earned this completely on your own merits."

She looked into his eyes for a long moment and then nodded. "I believe you."

Their coffees arrived, and she tipped a packet of sugar into her cappuccino. He watched her hands as they worked—as efficient and graceful with a sugar packet as they were with flowers. What would they be like on his body? Fluttering over his neck and collarbone. Trailing a path down his chest, his abdomen.

He tore his gaze away and stirred cream into his own coffee. "Did you turn the job down because you thought you hadn't earned it?"

That fitted the emerging profile of this woman, but she shook her head.

"I don't want a desk job."

"But you want your career to go places," he pointed out.

"The places I want to go are filled with flowers and customers."

He took a sip of his coffee and replaced the cup on its saucer, giving himself a moment to think the situation through. "I honestly thought you'd want this job."

She frowned, her head tilted to the side. "If you'd wanted to do something nice for me, instead of doing something you thought I'd like, you could have done what I asked for in the first place."

"Put one of your designs in the catalog of standard arrangements." It seemed obvious now, but hindsight was twenty-twenty.

"Bingo." She lifted her coffee cup to her lips, smiling over the rim, her dimples peeking out.

He regarded her as she took a sip and then ran her tongue over her bottom lip to catch a droplet. In her vivid purple dress and with the smattering of pale freckles over her nose, she was the brightest thing in the whole café, as if her own personal beam of sunshine followed her around and shone down on her wherever she was. Yet the arrangement she'd made for him to consider had been as conservative as they came. It was a contradiction he wanted to understand.

He leaned back in the booth and interlaced his fingers on the table. "Why did you show me such a conservative design that night? It's not who you are."

For a brief second, her eyes widened. "Who am I?"

He thought back to the first time he'd met her, near the stage at the auction, to the night he'd kissed her, to the day he'd watched her work in his store. "You're crab apple, carnation and mint bouquets. You're mixing wild colors with flair that's uncommon. You're edgy and fresh." And so much more. "Why didn't you show me any of that?"

Her eyes lit from within. "I didn't think you'd want to see that. I thought you'd prefer more conservative designs, like the ones already in the catalog."

"But that's the point." He leaned forward, wanting her to understand this if nothing else. "We already have designs like that. We don't have *your* designs. Hawke's Blooms needs your vision."

An adorable pink flush stole over her face, from her neck up to her cheekbones. "So, you're not mad I turned the job down?"

"Mad? No." He rubbed two fingers across his forehead. "It was my fault—I leapt ahead without talking to you. With any other employee, I would have researched first, found out what they wanted before making a decision."

"So, why didn't you?" she asked, her voice soft.

Good question—one he'd been asking himself. And she deserved the real answer. "To be honest, you've had me off center from the start."

She gave him a rueful smile. "I know how that feels."

He smiled back, and their gazes held for one heartbeat, two. Part of him was glad he wasn't the only one off kilter—that it was the result of some inconvenient mutual chemistry—but another part of him wished it had been more one-sided. That he could justify to himself that reaching across the table for her now would be an unwelcome advance, and reinforce that he had to keep his hands to himself.

What they needed was a new start. He drew in a deep breath and pushed his cup to the side. "How about we forget the promotion and you continue working in this store for now. I know the customers here will be glad to keep you."

"I'd like that," she said with a quick nod.

She glanced in the direction of her store, and a thought suddenly occurred to him. This wouldn't be a new start for her—he already suspected Faith's manager might resent her, and now she'd be heading back into that same environment after turning down a promotion. That could get awkward fast. He'd made a complete mess of this from start to finish.

"You know," he said, thinking on his feet, "another option is to move to a different store. I can think of a few managers who'd welcome someone with your skills and ability to form rapport with customers."

"Thank you, I appreciate the offer but I'm happy here." She turned her wrist over and checked her watch. "Speaking of which, I'd better get back."

He resisted a chuckle. Many of his employees would try to drag out their one-on-one time with him, especially if they'd already spent money on an opportunity to impress him. Not Faith. "You realize you're out with the person in charge of the entire chain of stores, right? You're not playing hooky."

She shook her head, unmoved by his reasoning. "We have a lot of orders to fill before I clock off."

"What time do you finish today?" he asked, an idea forming in his head as he said the words.

"Three o'clock."

"That's in two hours. How about I pick you up then and we go on our second date?" Since she wouldn't let him buy the dates back from her, it was probably better to get them out of the way as soon as was practical.

"Sure," she said as she stood. "But do me a favor and

don't come back to the store. It won't help my popularity in there."

It was a reasonable point. He liked that she thought that way. She could have used the opportunity to gain points against her manager, perhaps engage in a game of one-upmanship, but he'd come to see that wasn't the way Faith operated.

He pushed a paper napkin across the table and took a pen from the inside pocket of his jacket. "Give me your address and I'll drop by your place at about three-thirty."

She leaned over and wrote her address on the napkin before pushing it back to him and leaving.

He watched her walk out, taking in the sway of her hips as she moved, and then looked down at the napkin in his hand. After her address, she'd written four words. *I like the beach.*

A grin spread across his face. He was already looking forward to this afternoon way too much.

# Four

By three-twenty, Faith was waiting at her front door. She wanted to be ready to dash down the front steps when Dylan arrived because the last thing she needed was him knocking on her door. Being alone with him would lead to the possibility of her dragging him inside and repeating that kiss. And knowing there was a bed in the next room couldn't be good in that situation...

The beach suggestion had come from the same train of thought—she knew they had to go somewhere public. Though she'd also wanted it to be informal so she had a chance to question him casually and get more insight into what he was looking for with the catalog, to make her next attempt more likely to succeed. She had high hopes of getting the information while sitting next to him on the sand and not having to look him in the eye.

At three twenty-seven, his Porsche convertible drew

up, and she pulled her front door shut behind her, hiked her beach bag higher on her shoulder and jogged down the concrete stairs to the road. She loved the idea of owning a convertible, of having the wind in her hair as she drove, but the sheer expense of the model Dylan owned simply served to reinforce the differences between them.

"Have you got your swimsuit in that bag?" he asked as she slid into the passenger seat.

Was he kidding? Being half-naked in his presence could be disastrous. And seeing him in board shorts, his bare chest dripping with water…? Yeah, that was only going to lead to trouble. Whether they'd be in public or not, her willpower had its limits.

Though, she thought as she glanced over and took in the red-and-white-striped T-shirt that bunched around his biceps and stretched across his shoulders, perhaps his covered chest wasn't going to be much easier to cope with.

She faced the windshield and shrugged. "I was thinking more along the lines of sitting on a towel with the sand between my toes."

"That sounds safer," he said as he pulled away from the curb.

So he was still having trouble, too. Interesting. They talked about the weather and made other small talk until he found a park and they stepped out into the sunshine.

He looked down at her Hawaiian print bag. "Did you bring a towel, or should I get the picnic blanket?"

"You keep a picnic blanket in your car?" She couldn't help the smile—it seemed such a sweet thing for a playboy like Dylan to do. Although maybe he used it to seduce women under the stars…? Her smile faded.

"My brother Liam and I took his daughters, Bonnie and Meg, for a picnic a couple of weeks ago. The blanket is still in the back."

Her smile returned. She'd read the newspaper stories about Liam Hawke's engagement to Princess Jensine of Larsland—everybody had—and seen the photos of Liam's tiny baby, Bonnie, and Jenna's daughter, Meg, who was only a few months older than Bonnie. She just hadn't quite imagined Dylan actually interacting with the little girls. Which was probably unfair—by all accounts, the three brothers were close.

She hitched the bag over her shoulder. "No, I have a towel."

He nodded and set the keyless lock. They found a spot on the white sand to spread out her towel. The beach was fairly quiet, so there was no one else close enough to hear them, but there were still people around—people swimming in the sparkling blue Pacific, a couple of guys throwing a Frisbee back and forth, couples on towels farther away, occasional joggers.

Dylan slipped off his shoes and rolled up his chinos before sitting at the other end of the towel, leaving plenty of space between them. She wasn't facing him, which was supposed to be safe, yet her attention seemed to be located on his bare ankles, which she could see out of the corner of her eye. Why had she never noticed how attractive men's ankles were before? Or was it something special about this man's?

She swallowed hard and brought her focus back to her career. These dates were for her career.

"Mr. Hawke, you—"

"Dylan," he said, interrupting her. "'Dylan' is fine when we're alone."

"Are you sure?" A light breeze toyed with the hair that had escaped her clip, so she tucked it behind her ear. "If we become personal, won't we risk…?" She didn't know how to end that sentence, so she left it hanging.

He pulled his legs up and rested his forearms on his bent knees. "I hardly think using my first name will lead to me leaping on top of you here on the towel. Besides, 'Mr. Hawke' is too formal for the beach."

As soon as he'd said the words *me leaping on top of you*, she had trouble drawing breath. For a long moment, she couldn't get past the image of him above her, feeling his weight pushing her into the sand. She bit down on her bottom lip, hard. It seemed that he was right—using his first name wasn't the problem since she hadn't said it yet.

"Okay. Dylan." She gathered a handful of towel and the sand beneath it and gripped tight, as if she could draw strength from the beach itself. "You mentioned that the catalog didn't have anything like the designs you saw me do when you were at the store."

"That's true," he said, his voice deep and smooth. "We don't have anything like them."

She twisted around a little so she could see his eyes, but more importantly, so he could see hers and know she was serious about this. "Will you give me another chance to submit a design? One that's more…*me*?"

A slow smile spread across his face, and he nodded once. "I was hoping you'd still want to submit. Hawke's Blooms needs at least one Faith Crawford design between the covers of its catalog."

"Thank you," she said, excitement building inside. She'd been pretty sure he'd be open to looking at another arrangement, but even so, she hadn't wanted to count her chickens before they hatched. This time she'd blow his socks off.

"But," he said, "explain this to me, because I still don't understand. You're ambitious enough to use your savings to get access to me, yet you don't want a promotion." His expression was curious. It didn't feel as if the man who'd offered her the promotion was asking this time—it was more like a friend asking.

She looked out over the blue Pacific Ocean, the sound of the waves crashing on the shore lulling her into feeling at ease. "I like working with flowers. Flowers make people happy. They make *me* happy."

"So, what do you want out of your career, Faith?" His voice was soft near her ear, but she didn't turn, just watched the rhythmic pounding of the waves.

"I want to keep growing as a florist, to move on to new experiences and places, to be doing bigger and better arrangements all the time." She risked a glance at him, wondering if she dared tell him the size of her dreams. She'd never told a soul—had always been scared people would laugh at her.

"There's more, isn't there?" he asked, his gaze encouraging.

There was something about him looking at her like that. He could ask her anything and she'd probably tell him. She nodded. "One day, my arrangements will grace important places, large-scale events—they'll reach hundreds, maybe hundreds of thousands of people and bring them happiness."

One side of his mouth pulled into a lopsided grin. She looked back at the waves crashing on the shore and the children building sand castles. "You probably think that's silly."

From her peripheral vision she saw him reach out as if to run a hand down her arm, but he let it drop a moment before he touched her. She felt his gaze, however, remain trained on her. "I think it's amazing."

"You're not teasing?" she asked, turning to him, hardly daring to breathe. She wanted so badly for him to be telling the truth.

"I've heard a lot of reasons that people have chosen floristry before, and most of them were really good. But I think yours is my favorite." His voice was soft, intimate. Despite sharing the beach with countless other people, it was as if they were completely alone on the towel. From a distance, they might look like any couple together for an afternoon, and the idea was exhilarating.

"Thank you," she whispered.

There was silence for a long moment when all she could hear was her own breath. Then Dylan rubbed a hand down his face and sat a little straighter. "So is there a destination for your life's plan? Somewhere in particular you're headed?"

She picked up a handful of sand and let it fall through her fingers. "Not really." In fact, the idea of reaching a destination made her uneasy. "I guess I'm more comfortable staying on the move."

"Hmm… There's more to that answer, isn't there?"

She looked up, startled that he'd seen through her. Again. Then she nodded. "I've moved so much in my life, changing everything each time, that I've become something of a rolling stone."

"That makes me wonder, Faith Sixty-Three." He raised an eyebrow. "Are you moving all the time because you want to, or are you worried that if you stop, you'll sink?"

She laughed softly. "That's ridiculous. I move because I want to. I like my life this way."

But was that true? Something inside her tensed at the thought. Perhaps she was more comfortable choosing to move on, being a step ahead of anyone who might make her leave. That little girl who was always waiting for the axe to fall was still inside her. A cold shiver ran down her spine. Honestly, she was only comfortable if she decided to move on her own terms—jumping before she was pushed. If she jumped, she was in control of the situation, so since she'd become an adult, she'd been jumping from place to place. So far she'd avoided being pushed away.

Not that she'd ever admit that to Dylan Hawke—she'd pretty much reached her limit on sharing. Yet this was still the most open she'd been with anyone, and it didn't scare her the way it usually did. Why was that, exactly?

She took in his strong profile, his dark hair that was moving in the gentle breeze, the day-old stubble that covered his jaw. She felt safe with him.

"You know," she said, feeling this was something that he *should* know. "I haven't told anyone this before. About being a rolling stone."

His green eyes softened. "Thank you for sharing it with me." His forehead crumpled into lines and he swallowed. "And it seems only fair that I repay your honesty in kind."

"Yes?" she said and held her breath.

"The night we met, you asked if I'd ever had a dream of my own." His voice was stilted, as if he hadn't put these thoughts into words before. "I didn't answer you, but the truth is, no. The only dreams I can remember having are the dreams I have in common with my family for our business." His gaze was piercing, looking deep within her. "Are you shocked?"

She swallowed hard to get her voice to work. "I'm honored you shared that with me."

"And if we're being completely honest," he said, his chest rising and falling faster than it had only minutes ago, "I have to tell you that I've never wanted to kiss a woman more than I do in this moment. But I can't let myself."

She squeezed her eyes shut against the truth, but he deserved to know he wasn't alone. Deliberately she opened her eyes again and met his gaze. "I've never wanted to kiss a man this much, either. Ever since the moment our lips first touched, I've been thinking about doing it again."

He groaned and let his head fall into his hands. "I'm not sure if I prefer knowing that, or if it was easier not thinking you felt the same."

She sighed, understanding how he felt. "You're not the only one feeling the chemistry. But I don't want to act on it, either."

Without looking up, he reached across the towel and intertwined their hands. The slide of his skin against her fingers made her breath hitch. Holding his hand was such a poor substitute for what she really wanted, but it would have to be enough.

Dylan refused to look down at where his fingers were wrapped around Faith's. If he acknowledged it, he'd have to break the contact.

What were they doing at the beach, anyway? She'd been clear from the start that she'd bought the time with him to help her career. Since this was their second date, he should be doing something for her career now.

Reaching a decision, he released her hand and jumped to his feet. "Come on. There's somewhere I want to take you."

She looked up at him warily. "Where?"

Her meaning hit him—he'd said he wanted to kiss her and then held her hand. It was natural she would think that next he might push the boundaries further. "It's job-related, I promise."

He held out his hand again, but this time it was to help her up. She took it and he pulled her up to stand in front of him. She was so close he could feel her body heat. She smelled of flowers, which was no surprise given that she'd been handling them all day, but also of strawberries. His gaze dropped to her lips, which had a slick of red gloss coating them. She was wearing strawberry lip gloss. His pulse spiked, imagining the flavor when he kissed her.

Abruptly she released his hand and stepped back. "You said we were going somewhere job-related?"

He picked up the towel and shook it with more force than was necessary before answering. "I want you to see the Hawke's Blooms flower farm."

Her eyes lit with the same passion she'd shown when she talked about her future. "I'd love that!"

As they walked back to the car, then drove out of LA to San Juan Capistrano, where the farm was located, she peppered him with questions about the farm's capacity and stock.

"Have you always had it out here?" she asked once they drew close.

He nodded. "We moved here when I was a kid. My

parents had been farmers, so when they came out to California, they tried their hand at growing flowers. They wanted something that would give their three sons opportunities and thought this was the way to do it."

"From your success, I'd say they were right." Her voice held no trace of flattery. It was an honest observation, and it had more weight for it.

"Yeah," he said, allowing satisfaction about the business he'd built with his family to fill his chest. He owed his parents more than he could ever repay. Not that they wanted anything other than to see their sons happy and thriving, but he'd find a way to show them how grateful he was one day.

"So, whose idea was it to sell the flowers as well as grow them?" Faith asked.

"We had a roadside stall when we started." He smiled at the memory. "Dad would sell to the flower markets, but every weekend, Adam and I would go with Mom and sell whatever we had left."

"What about your other brother?"

He chuckled. "Liam prefers plants to people, so he'd stay home with Dad. And it's a good thing he did—it was Liam's breakthroughs with new flowers that put us on the map."

"I was really impressed with his Midnight Lily. The customers have been loving it."

"It's a great flower," Dylan said, feeling a surge of pride. The new blue lily had been launched a couple of months earlier and had been selling like crazy ever since.

She lifted one foot up, rested it on the seat and wrapped an arm around her knee. "So you and your other brother were stuck selling by the roadside?"

"There were three of us there, but the sales came down to our mom and me. Adam always saw himself in a more...managerial role." Adam had set himself up behind the stall in what Dylan and his mother had called "Adam's office."

Out of the corner of his eye, he saw her cock her head to the side. "How much management does a road-side stall need?"

"Even though I teased him about trying to get out of work, he probably worked harder than any of us. He made posters and put them on stakes by the road, ex-perimented with price points and kept a chart of the sales so he could work out what to stock. During the week, he was always doing something to our stall, too. Either painting it a different color to see if that attracted more people, or constructing new benches for the flower buckets from wood he salvaged."

"Sounds like quite the entrepreneur." There was a smile in her voice.

"He is," Dylan said with no small measure of affec-tion. "That's why Liam and I let Adam run the over-all company. Liam's happier with his plants, anyway."

"And you?" Her voice grew soft. "What do you pre-fer?"

He shrugged one shoulder. "I'm more of a people person. I like the buzz of retail. The colors of it. I like talking to staff and customers—interacting."

"I can see that about you," she said, her tone pensive.

"When we opened our first store, my mother and I staffed it." They'd been amazing times, full of energy and excitement. "Liam and Dad were back home grow-ing the plants and drawing scientific charts of plant breeding, and Adam was in his room, making spreadsheets and plans. My job was more fun."

"To you. But I'll bet to them, your job sounded like hell."

He grinned. "Actually, yes. Being in a room full of people has been known to make them both yearn for their charts and spreadsheets."

He pulled into the drive to Liam's place and went through security. It had been tightened now that Liam was engaged to a princess, and Dylan was glad for the little girls' sakes.

"This looks more like a private residence," Faith said warily.

"Liam still lives on-site. It's the same house we grew up in, actually, though he's had so much work done to it, you'd never know."

"But there was a specific farm entrance before this driveway," she said, pointing.

"If I came all the way out here and didn't tell him, he'd kill me. Well," he amended as he thought about what he'd said, "he probably wouldn't notice, but his fiancée definitely would kill me. We'll only be there a minute or two—just passing through."

"Hang on—" she put her hands on the dashboard as if she could slow their approach "—you're taking me to meet his fiancée?"

"If that's okay with you," Dylan said, glancing over at her. He hadn't thought she might be uncomfortable—Faith always seemed as if she was ready for any adventure life threw at her.

Her mouth opened and closed again before she replied. "She's a princess!"

"As it turns out, yes." He wanted to smile at the awe

in her voice, but he restrained himself. He'd known Jenna before he'd found out she was a princess, so he hadn't had a chance to be overwhelmed by her royal status. However, he understood that this was probably an intimidating situation for Faith to be thrown into with no warning. He had confidence that she'd cope—he couldn't imagine anything overwhelming Faith for long.

Her expression was still uncertain as he pulled up in front of the house. But he wasn't driving out here without at least saying hello to little Bonnie and Meg.

He walked around to open her door. "Are you coming?"

"Are there protocols about what I should say?" she asked as she climbed out.

He shrugged one shoulder casually. "I'd go with complimenting their daughters and being particularly nice to me."

"You?"

"What can I say? The princess is fond of me."

She narrowed her eyes at him as she realized he was teasing, but she'd lost the slightly awed look, which was what he'd been aiming for.

Jenna met them at the door, twelve-month-old Meg on her hip. "Dylan," she said in her lilting Scandinavian accent, "what a nice surprise."

He kissed her cheek, took Meg from her and held her up in the air until he elicited a giggle, and then kissed her cheek as well. "I'm not here long. We're on our way down to see Liam and stopped by to say hello first."

"Liam's in his office, working on his latest project. In the meantime," she said, taking Meg back, "why don't you introduce me to your friend?"

"Jenna, this is Faith. She's a florist at our Santa Monica store." He didn't need to emphasize the point. Jenna knew as well as any of them that he couldn't get involved with one of their florists. "Faith, this is my future sister-in-law, Jenna."

Jenna held out her hand. To Faith's credit, she hesitated only a moment before accepting it. "Lovely to meet you," Faith said.

Jenna smiled, and he could see her brain working overtime, trying to work out if there was something going on between them. She was far too insightful. "Would you like a drink before you set out?"

Faith shook her head, and he wanted to get moving and focused on work again before Jenna could corner him with awkward questions. "We're fine."

"Do you mind if we come with you? Bonnie is still napping, and our housekeeper can keep an ear out for her. I haven't been outside the house all day, and I'd like Meg to get some fresh air and see something other than me."

"That would be great." And it would keep him on his best behavior. None of those intimate moments they'd accidentally had at the beach.

Five minutes later, they were walking out the back door.

"It's huge," Faith said, looking out across the fields of brightly colored blooms. "Do you use them all?"

"The main purpose is to stock our own shops," he said as he opened the small gate that marked the edge of Liam's yard, "but we sell the excess to other stores at the flower markets."

They followed a paved path to a building off to the side—Liam's pride and joy. The Hawke's Blooms research facility.

When they went through the sliding doors, Jenna lifted Meg from the stroller and carried her in her arms, and Dylan spoke to a woman at the front desk. "Can you let Liam know that I'm here to see him, please?"

She put a call through, and then looked back to him. "He's on his way down."

Dylan dug his hands into his pockets and glanced over at Faith as she made baby talk with Meg. He had another plan in mind to help her career, and this time he'd be sure to take it slow and check that she was on board first. But despite his caution, he had a very good feeling about this particular plan. And that made him happier than he should have been comfortable with.

# Five

Faith was aware that Princess Jensine of Larsland was studying her, and she had to resist squirming. It seemed almost surreal that a small-town girl who'd spent her entire childhood being shunted from one relative to another should find herself face-to-face with a member of royalty.

"You look familiar," Jenna eventually said. "Have we met before?"

Dylan cleared his throat. "You might have seen her at the auction," he admitted. "Faith had the winning bid on a date with me."

Jenna's eyes widened. "This is a date? You brought a *date* to a research lab?"

"It's not like that," Faith said quickly. "Besides, even if we wanted to, we couldn't have a real date because of company policy."

She covered her mouth with two fingers. Had she just admitted she would have liked to date Dylan if the situation had been different? No one else seemed to have taken it that way. But she needed to stay on her guard because, deep down, there wasn't much in the world she would want more than for Dylan to kiss her again, and she didn't want anyone—especially Dylan—guessing that.

"Ah, yes," Jenna said. One corner of her mouth turned up. "That old fraternization policy. I know it well."

Liam pushed through the door into the waiting room and beamed when he saw his fiancée. He took Meg from her, swung her around onto his hip and kissed Jenna softly. "Hi," he said.

"Hi, yourself," she said back and kissed him again.

Dylan coughed loudly. "Hey, other people present."

Liam looked up but pulled Jenna under his arm. It was only then that he seemed to register there was a stranger in the room. He released Jenna and stuck out a hand. "I'm Liam Hawke, since it seems my brother isn't going to introduce us."

"I'm Faith Crawford," she said, straightening her spine as she shook his hand. "I work for you."

"You do?" Liam asked, his head cocked to the side.

Dylan took a step closer to her elbow. She could feel his body heat. "Faith is a florist at the Santa Monica store."

"Okay, good to meet you," Liam said.

Jenna looked up at her man, her eyes full of mischief. "Faith won Dylan at the auction."

Dylan held up a hand. "She didn't win me." His gaze darted to Faith before turning back to his brother. "She had the winning bid on some *time* with me."

"Three dates," Jenna supplied helpfully.

"They're not dates, just time," Dylan clarified. "In fact, this is some of that time now. Faith has a lot of creativity in her designs, and we've identified her as someone with potential. So I wanted to show her around the building."

"Sure," Liam said casually, holding Dylan's gaze. "The public areas?"

"Up to you," Dylan said just as casually.

Faith looked from one to the other, trying to work out what they were really saying. It was obvious something else was being discussed, but what?

"You'll vouch for her discretion?" Liam asked.

Dylan nodded. "I'm willing to bet on it."

"Then you're about to." Liam looked up at Faith and smiled. "Welcome to my world. Let me show you around."

It seemed she'd passed some kind of test on Dylan's say-so, but she had no idea what it had been for. They spent the next twenty minutes walking through the research rooms, and Faith was enthralled with all the projects they had going on. Crossbreeding for stronger scent or bigger flowers, rooms full of benches with lines of pots containing grafted plants. Excitement buzzed through her blood at seeing the powerhouse behind the business.

Then they reached a locked door. Liam caught her gaze. "Past this door is my personal project. Very few people know what's in here, and even fewer have seen it. If we go inside, I need your word that you won't leak the information."

"You have my word," she said without hesitation.

Liam looked to Dylan, who nodded, and opened the door.

The room was like many of the others in that it had

benches with rows of pots, each containing plants at different stages of growth. But the flower that many of the pots had was like nothing in the other rooms. Or anything she'd seen before. Faith knew flowers. She knew the conditions they preferred and their shelf lives. She knew which flowers were in season at any given time in which area of the country. She knew what colors each variety came in. But she'd never seen anything like the flower in those pots.

She stepped closer. It was an iris, but it was a rich red. She wanted to touch it but was unsure, so she looked up at Liam. "May I?"

He nodded his permission. With her fingertip, she touched the petal of one of the more advanced flowers. "It's beautiful," she breathed.

"Thank you," Liam said.

Dylan moved to her elbow. "How do you think it will go with the customers?"

She lifted her head and found his deep green gaze. "I think we'll be stampeded." She meant it. There was nothing like this flower on the market, and it was stunning. Already she could imagine how perfect it would look in a bridal bouquet or dramatic table decoration. Its crimson bloom would be the center of attention.

"Tell me, Faith," Dylan said, crossing his arms over his broad chest, "what would you put with it to showcase it?"

"The design would need to be simple. It's so beautiful, it doesn't need much adornment. Perhaps something with soft white petals, like old-fashioned roses. Maybe a touch of silver foliage."

Dylan gave her an indulgent smile and dug his hands in his pockets. "Do you want a chance to try?"

"Make an arrangement with one of these?" she asked, her heart racing with excitement. "Now?"

Dylan lifted an eyebrow at Liam, who nodded. "Yep, now. We'll wait here while you go out to the farm. Collect whatever you want. Then come back and make us an arrangement."

Chest almost bursting, Faith nodded and threaded her way back to the door.

As soon as Faith was gone, Dylan looked to his brother. "Thanks."

"If you believe in her, then that's enough for me. But," he said, his voice becoming serious, "do you know what you're doing? She's an employee."

Dylan arched an eyebrow. "That didn't stop the two of you."

"It did for a little while," Jenna said, grinning up at Liam.

Liam returned the grin and then said, "It was different for us. Jenna was working for me personally, not the company."

Dylan leaned back on the bench. He'd had enough of this topic of conversation. The last thing he needed was for them to discover he'd crossed the line in a spectacular fashion on the very first night by kissing her.

He shook his head once. "There's nothing to worry about. I'm just being a good boss and giving opportunities to someone with potential."

"Sure you are," Jenna said and winked.

"How are Bonnie and Meg?" Dylan asked, hoping the new topic would sidetrack them both for the short while it took Faith to return.

"They're just perfect," Jenna said, a dreamy look of contentment on her face.

Dylan asked Jenna a few more questions about the girls and suggested Liam find some floral tools for Faith to keep them occupied. Finally there was a call from the front desk, and Liam told them to let Faith back through.

She entered with her arms full of flowers, her bright red hair falling from the clip she'd used to try to tame her curls. Dylan jumped up to help, taking some of the blooms and spreading them across a vacant bench.

"Here, you might need these," he said, passing her the box of tools. As their fingers brushed, he felt a tingle of electricity shoot up his arm, but he did his best to ignore it. This was a professional situation, and even if it weren't, she was still an employee, as Liam had just pointed out.

After recapturing her hair in the clip, Faith began to work with the flowers, trimming the thorns and leaves from the white roses, using floral wire on the blush-pink gerbera daisies and arranging them together. Liam cut three of his red irises and handed them to her.

The expression in Faith's eyes, of awe and honor, made Dylan's heart swell in his chest. Her passion was contagious—he felt alive, as if every cell in his body was waking up.

"Thank you," she said as she took the flowers from Liam, her voice breathless. Then she wove the other flowers around them, creating a design that was elegant in its simplicity, yet stunning.

When she was finished, she held the bouquet out to Dylan. He smiled as he took it and then showed it to Jenna and Liam.

"What do you think?" he asked his brother and soon-to-be sister-in-law. They knew what he was really asking—they'd begun talks already about launching the new flower on the market with an event, in the same way they'd launched the Midnight Lily a few months ago. Jenna had been the brains behind that and it had been a roaring success. They'd already started on preliminary plans for the second launch, and Jenna had asked him to supply a florist from his staff to work on it part-time.

Jenna turned to Liam, one eyebrow raised, and he nodded. Then she turned to Faith.

"Faith," she said, her musical voice soft. "What would you say to working part-time with me on the launch of the new iris? I need a florist to handle the arrangements and a few other duties, and we think you'd be perfect."

Faith looked from Jenna to Dylan, eyes wide. Wary about pushing her into a job she didn't want again, he explained further. "If you want to do it, we'll work your hours at the store around this. You could do part-time at each until the launch, then go back to full-time at the store."

"Then I'd love to," she said, her warm brown eyes sparkling, and Dylan felt the satisfaction of a good plan coming together.

Jenna grinned. "Great. I have to take Meg back up to the house, but I'll be in touch about the details."

As they drove away a short while later, Dylan glanced over at Faith. He wanted to make sure this was really what she wanted, especially after he'd botched things the last time he'd tried to help her career.

"Faith, I want you to know that this is totally up to you. If you'd enjoy the work, we'd love to have you on the project. But you can still change your mind, and it won't affect your job at the Santa Monica store."

She gave him a beaming smile. "Honestly, I can't thank you enough. The opportunity of doing large arrangements that will be seen by hundreds of people is a dream come true. And Jenna seems lovely—I think I'll enjoy working with her."

As he stopped at a red light, he glanced over and found Faith looking at him as if he'd hung the moon. His heart clenched tight. He had a bad feeling that, despite everything, he'd do whatever it took to keep that look on her face. The light turned green, and he trained his gaze on the road ahead, shoring up the strength to do the right thing.

One week into her new working life, Faith looked up from the arrangement she was making to find Dylan letting himself in through the door of the secure room where they were keeping the new flower a secret from the world.

As he crossed over to her, she bit down on a smile, unwilling to let it escape. He was earlier than expected, and that made her happier than it should have. Of course, every time she saw him—no, every time she even thought about him—it made her happier than it should. And yet it also made her sadder, since this was one man she shouldn't be thinking about, or daydreaming about, in the first place. Her reactions to him were stronger than they should have been to a boss, and somehow she had to find a way to contain that.

This week she'd been designing arrangements with the new iris for the Hawke's Blooms promotions team to use for posters and media releases after the official launch. To give them enough lead time for their own design work, she'd agreed this would be her first priority. It hadn't been a problem to work quickly—she was bursting with ideas. She'd even suggested they call the new flower the Ruby Iris, and everyone had liked the name. She loved that this flower would permanently have a little piece of her attached to it.

And this afternoon, a panel of the three Hawke brothers and Jenna would choose the two arrangements to send the publicity team from six Faith had made. Her stomach had been filled with butterflies all day.

"Hey, Dylan," she said when he reached her. "I didn't expect you for another hour, when the rest of the panel is coming."

He dug his hands into his trouser pockets. "I had a bit of time on my hands and thought I'd stop by in case you needed any last-minute help."

"You've already been a huge help."

He'd dropped in a couple of times already this week. She'd taken advantage of that time, peppering him with questions about the launch of the Midnight Lily, looking for details that would give her clues about what they'd be looking for this time. Dylan had answered all her questions. She wondered, though, if he was also keeping an eye on her—he'd suggested her for this job, so if she messed it up, it would reflect badly on him.

He made himself busy clearing the bench where she'd been working.

"You don't have to do that," she said, her gaze on the white iris in her hand. "I've left enough time to clean up before the others arrive."

He flashed her a smile. "But I'm here. I may as well do something to help."

She paused, watching him clearing the bench with bold, sweeping movements, fixing things. Making things better for her. Dylan Hawke was a mystery in many ways. She'd worked for several florists and had quite a few bosses over the years, but never had she found any who were happy to roll up their sleeves and get their hands dirty. They usually preferred to have their underlings do the menial tasks.

She popped the flower back into the jug of water and turned so she could see him more clearly. "Why is it that you're the only boss I've ever had who was willing to do this?"

His broad shoulders lifted, then dropped, as if it were no big deal. "Someone's got to do it. Don't see why it shouldn't be me."

"Because your time is more valuable." He opened his mouth, and she could tell there was a denial on his tongue, so she held up a hand. "Seriously, your hourly rate must dwarf mine."

"I might get paid more, but I can't create something like that," he said, gesturing to the design she had almost finished. But there was something else in his eyes, something he wasn't admitting to.

She crossed her arms under her breasts. "Tell me what the rest of that story is."

"Don't you have work to do?" He tried to frown, but the corners of his mouth were twitching.

"Conveniently, someone just cleaned up my work area, so now I have a few extra minutes to play with. And I'd like to spend them hearing the real story behind the line you just tried to feed me."

"A line?" His hand went to his heart. "You wound me."

"Wow," she said, hoisting herself up to sit on the

bench. "You really don't want to talk about this, do you?"

He arched an eyebrow, leaning on the bench only a hand span away. "You really want to know the truth?"

"Yeah, I really do."

Something changed in his face, his demeanor. She couldn't quite put her finger on it, but she knew without a doubt that he was baring himself to her. Trusting her. The knowledge squeezed her heart tight.

"Truth is," he said, his voice deep, "lately I've been thinking about the buzz I used to get, setting up the original stores. Working with customers and having a new challenge were what got me out of bed in the mornings."

"Your job now must have challenges." Being the head of the Hawke's Blooms stores sounded as if it would be pretty much all challenge.

"Sure. But there was a joy back then that doesn't exist now." He ran his hands through his already rumpled hair. "I'm not sure how to explain it exactly, but in the old days, when my family was first starting the company, we never knew what each day would bring. I can glimpse that excitement again when I watch you work."

Dylan looked into Faith's trusting brown eyes. There was another part to the answer that he dared not say aloud—he found that excitement again not only by watching her work but also by being around her. He never knew what she'd say or do next, and it was the most refreshing thing he'd experienced in a long time.

A knock on the door drew him out of his thoughts. He looked up to see his oldest brother, Adam, poking his head around the door. He suddenly realized how close he was standing to Faith and took a step to the side.

As Adam made his way over to them, his face was blank, but after a lifetime of knowing him, Dylan could read the question in his eyes.

"Liam and Jenna aren't here yet," Dylan said by way of a greeting—he'd spoken to Adam a couple of times today already, so a greeting seemed superfluous.

"That's okay," Adam replied. "It gives me a moment to meet our star florist."

Again, Adam's outward facade—politeness this time—didn't match what was going on underneath. He had sensed something and had every intention of getting to the bottom of it. Dylan squared his shoulders.

"Adam, this is Faith Crawford. Faith, this is Adam, the CEO of Hawke's Blooms Enterprises, which is the overall company that encompasses the stores, the farm and the markets."

Faith stuck out her hand, and Dylan didn't think his brother noticed the slight tremble as she shook his hand. "Good to meet you, Mr. Hawke."

"You'll have to call me Adam, or this meeting is going to get very confused with the three Mr. Hawkes together at once."

"Oh, of course." Her eyes darted to Dylan. "Thank you, Adam."

Dylan looked back at the bench and realized Faith wasn't quite finished with the last arrangement—he'd made her lose precious minutes. He swore under his breath.

He turned to his brother. "How about we give Faith a few minutes to make the last touches before the others arrive?"

"Sure. There are a few things I wanted to discuss with you, anyway."

As they headed for the door, Dylan threw Faith a smile over his shoulder, and she mouthed "thank you" back to him. Knowing her, even once she'd added the final couple of flowers, she'd want a few minutes on her own to get her head together without worrying about a new Hawke brother watching her.

Once the door closed behind them, Adam said, "Coffee?"

"Excellent plan."

The staff room was empty, and Dylan headed for the coffee machine, making an espresso each for himself and Adam.

"So, what's the deal with you and Faith?" Adam asked bluntly as he grabbed the sugar jar.

Dylan handed his brother a coffee. "Just helping an employee with potential to advance her career."

Adam sighed, but there was a smile lurking in his eyes. "Dylan, I've known you your entire life. I saw you when you had your first crush, and I drove you to the movies on your first date. Don't try to bullshit me. Your interest in that woman is more than an employer's."

Dylan leaned back on the counter. "It's really that obvious?"

"Maybe not to everyone, but to me? Yes." Adam moved closer and clapped him on the back. "What are you going to do?"

"I've got it under control."

"You call this under control?" Adam rolled his eyes to heaven as if appealing for help. "What happened when you kissed her?"

Caught off guard, Dylan felt as if he'd been sucker punched. "How do you know I kissed her?"

Adam's eyebrows shot up. "I didn't until you just confirmed it."

Realizing his mistake too late, Dylan groaned. "What you have to understand—"

"Oh, good. Stories that start this way are always juicy."

Ignoring him, Dylan started again. "What you have to understand is that we didn't meet at work. Well, not exactly."

Adam sipped his coffee. "You ran into an employee socially?"

"Remember that bachelor auction Jenna organized for our charity? The one you managed to wriggle out of being involved with?" he asked pointedly.

Uncharacteristically, Adam's gaze dropped to the floor. "I was, uh, busy that night."

"Sure you were," Dylan said, not believing it for a second. "Anyway, Faith placed the winning bid on me."

"You were bought by one of your florists?" Adam said, horrified.

"She bought some of my *time*," Dylan clarified.

Adam's expression didn't soften. "You've been out on a date with an employee?"

"No, she didn't want dates."

"What did she want?" he asked, his eyes narrowing.

"She asked me to meet her at the Santa Monica store and made a submission for the catalog."

"Did you accept it?"

"Nope."

"Her design wasn't even good enough for the book,

yet you have her here working on the most high-profile event in our history?"

"Her work is good. She deserves this spot, no question. The design she showed me that night was what she thought I wanted. When she does her own work, she's amazing."

"You said you wanted to rehabilitate your image. This won't help."

"It won't hurt, either, because nothing is going to happen."

"Sure. Let's get back to you kissing an employee."

"Yeah, I'd rather not. I'm trying to forget it."

"How's that working out for you?"

"Not as well as I'd like."

"Dylan," Adam said, shaking his head. "This is dangerous."

"I know."

"Do you? She seems nice, but if this goes badly for her, she can sue you. Hell, she can sue all of us because we have a policy that you've violated, but you're especially vulnerable."

"She's not like that. She wouldn't."

"You haven't known her long enough to be sure. You're the head of the chain of stores she works for, so she's been on her best behavior."

"I have no doubt that I've seen the real her."

"Now I'm even more worried. Is this woman really worth risking your career over? Exposing the entire company to legal action and a potential scandal?"

Liam poked his head around the door. "I thought I might find you two in here, stealing my coffee."

Dylan raised his mug. "You should have cookies in here, too."

Liam snorted a laugh. "Faith is ready if you are. Jenna's already in there."

Adam didn't move. "Come in here a minute and close the door."

Liam took the extra step inside the room and shut the door behind him. "What's up?"

Adam gestured in Dylan's direction. "Did you know about him kissing his florist?"

"Yes. Wait, no." He turned to Dylan. "You kissed her?"

"He kissed her," Adam confirmed, rocking back on his heels. "I'll brief the lawyers this afternoon in case we need to take preemptive action."

Dylan groaned. "Glad we're not overreacting."

Liam blew out a breath. "Look, I know things were different with me and Jenna, but I kissed her—heck, I made love to her—while she worked for me, and the world didn't end."

Dylan chuckled. "You sure acted as if it had ended there for a while. Remember that day we came over and—?"

Liam hit him upside the head. "I'm trying to help you, idiot."

"Uh, thanks?" Dylan said, rubbing his head.

Adam narrowed his eyes at them both. "You were lucky with Jenna. Most women in that situation would have reacted differently. Would have taken what they could get."

Dylan frowned at Liam. "Since when did he get so jaded about women?"

Liam shrugged a shoulder. "Many years ago. I always figured someone had broken his heart."

Adam threw up his hands. "I'm standing right here."

"Good point," Liam said. "So tell us who broke your heart? Was it Liz in college?"

"Nope," Dylan said. "He left her. I had to talk to her when she started calling the house, brokenhearted. Maybe it was—"

"Stop," Adam said in his oldest brother voice. "We're not discussing my dating history. We're talking about Dylan and the here and now."

"Actually," Liam said, "we're talking about which arrangements we want on the publicity materials. And two people are waiting for us." He opened the door and indicated the hallway with a hand. "Shall we?"

Adam straightened his tie, gave a last pointed look to Dylan and headed out.

"Thanks," Dylan said to Liam.

Liam nodded. "Just don't mess this up and get us into legal problems."

"I'll be careful," Dylan said and followed his brothers out the door, hoping like all hell he *was* capable of being careful around Faith Crawford.

# Six

From the corner of Liam's research lab, Faith watched the three Hawke brothers and Jenna as they walked around the designs she'd been working on all week. She'd been nervous the night she'd made the first arrangement for Dylan, but this was more intense. There was so much more riding on this verdict.

Finally Adam looked up and said, "Is everybody ready to make a decision?" The others nodded, so he continued. "I like number three. It's simple enough to work well in publicity, it keeps the focus on the iris and it's elegant, which will appeal to the public."

"Agreed," Liam said. "It's one of my top two choices as well."

They quickly settled on that arrangement and then had a robust discussion about the second choice, since the vote was split between two options.

As Faith watched the conversation, the excitement began to outweigh her nerves—the four of them were so animated about her designs. Her personal favorite hadn't been mentioned at all, and now that she'd heard the reasoning for their other choices, she could assume that her favorite was too cluttered to be effective in the posters. It was fascinating to hear the opinions of people more experienced than she was in this side of the flower business. In such a short time, she'd learned so much.

Once the decisions were made, all four of the panel members complimented Faith on her work, though it was Dylan's praise that made her heart swell. She tried not to watch him as the others spoke, tried to keep her reaction to him veiled, but there was a charisma that surrounded him, a magnetic force that drew her gaze back against her will.

Then Adam excused himself to rush off to a meeting, and Liam turned to Dylan. "Are you still okay to take them to the photographer's studio?"

"Sure," Dylan said. "I drove here in one of the refrigerated delivery vans. Faith, did you want to come to the photo shoot?"

Faith jerked her head up. She'd known they'd booked the photographer for this afternoon and that the chosen designs would be taken straight to the studio, but she'd been able to concentrate only on her part. She hadn't thought further than the panel arriving and assessing her work. Now, though, she could barely contain her enthusiasm about seeing the two successful designs photographed.

"I'd love to," she said, trying not to bounce on her toes. "If that's okay."

Jenna smiled. "Seems only fair that since you cre-ated them, you get to see it through."

"Then I'm in. I'll grab my bag."

While she gathered her things, Liam and Dylan sealed the two chosen arrangements plus a few single stems in boxes—since the new iris was still a secret—and carried them out to the delivery truck.

"What about my car?" Faith asked once the flowers were all loaded.

Dylan's green gaze flicked from her to her car. "Since your place is near the studio, how about I drop you home afterward, then bring you back out here in the morning for work?"

Jenna nodded. "This parking lot is secure overnight—the security gates will be shut and monitored."

"Okay, that sounds good then. Thank you."

"Not a problem," Dylan said as he opened her door for her. Her arm brushed his hand as she climbed in, sending a buzz of awareness through her body. He held her gaze for an instant, showing that he'd felt it, too. She pulled her seat belt over her shoulder and tried to pretend the moment of connection hadn't happened.

Once they'd set off on the road, he flashed her a grin. "So how did your nerves hold out? That must have been trying for you."

She tucked her legs up underneath her on the seat. "I have to admit, I was pretty tense while you were all judging, but it was thrilling, too. Thank you again for this opportunity."

"No, thank you," he said as he changed lanes to over-take a station wagon. "Even Adam liked your work, and he's hard to impress."

Her thoughts drifted back to seeing the three brothers together. They all looked so alike—tall and broad-shouldered, with thick, wavy hair the color of polished mahogany—yet so different at the same time. There was something…*more* in Dylan. An energy down deep in his soul, a passion for life that shone through in everything he did. In every move he made.

"I found Adam difficult to get a read on."

"That's Adam for you. He's what our mother calls 'self-contained.' Doesn't like sharing parts of himself if he can avoid it."

Curiosity made her turn to face Dylan. "Even with you and Liam?"

"Liam and I have found ways over the years to nudge him until he cracks." Dylan's expression changed—there was a touch of devilish mischief in the way his mouth quirked. "Some less fair than others."

"Like what?" she asked, intrigued.

"Oh, we just know what buttons to push." He grinned. "But we try to use our powers for good instead of evil. Most of the time we succeed."

Faith laughed. "Your powers are truly scary. I think I should be more careful around you."

There was silence for several heartbeats, and she felt the mood in the car—no, between *them*—change. Deepen.

"Pushing buttons isn't the reason you should be careful around me, Faith," he said, his voice like gravel.

Her skin heated. Even though she knew she shouldn't, she asked, "Why is it, then?"

"Because I start to lose perspective around you." He didn't look at her; his gaze remained focused on the road ahead, but she felt as if he was whispering in her ear.

"Sometimes I think you could crook your finger at me and I'd forget the company rules."

The breath caught in her throat. She was on the edge of a precipice, desperately wanting to fall, to let go, but she knew she couldn't. She swallowed hard and tried to make light of his comment. "Don't worry, I've never been able to master whistling, skipping or crooking a finger."

He laughed, but it sounded tight and unnatural. "Then we won't have a problem."

They talked about less loaded topics for the rest of the trip back to LA until they finally pulled up at the studio. They carried the boxes of arrangements and single stems to the front door, where the photographer was waiting for them.

"Come on in," she said. "The others are already here."

Dylan leaned over to whisper to Faith, "A couple of the publicity team members from Adam's office are meeting us here."

Once they were inside, the shoot seemed to move forward like clockwork. Dylan introduced her to the women from Hawke's Blooms' publicity team. Then she found a chair a few feet behind the camera and tried to stay out of the way.

Dylan, however, seemed to be the center of everything. His people management skills were on display, and in a charming, relaxed way, he was in total control of the photo shoot. She couldn't take her eyes off him. He exuded confidence, charisma and power. He raised an arm and everyone turned to see what he was pointing at. He called for assistance with something and several people rushed to help. He looked at her with his simmering gaze, and she practically swooned.

One of the publicity staff members, Amanda, took a seat next to her. "I can't wait to see how the photos turn out. You did some great work with those arrangements."

Faith felt the blush moving its way up her neck and was grateful that Amanda was watching the work in front of them and wouldn't notice. "Thank you. I'm looking forward to the photos as well."

"You're so lucky, getting to work with Dylan. All the girls in our office have a bit of a crush on him."

Faith tensed. Did Amanda know? Was she fishing? But the other woman still hadn't spared her a glance— if she'd been fishing, she would have been watching for a reaction.

Faith drew in an unsteady breath. "You all work for Adam, don't you?"

"Yep, and don't get me wrong. We love Adam, too. He's a great boss. But Dylan? He could charm the pants off just about anyone if he put his mind to it."

Faith felt the blush deepen and creep up to her cheeks. She didn't doubt that assessment in the least. Fortunately, Amanda didn't seem to be waiting for a reply.

"There's something about the way that man moves," Faith's new friend said. "You can tell he'd be a great lover."

Faith's heart skipped a beat. Just at that moment, Dylan glanced their way. He must have seen her looking a little flustered because he mouthed, "You okay?"

Amanda's words replayed in Faith's head, and she imagined lying naked with Dylan Hawke. Touching him without reserve. Being touched. Her mouth dried. Dylan frowned, taking a step toward her, and she realized she hadn't replied to him yet.

Summoning all her willpower, she found a smile and nodded, and he went back to overseeing the shoot. Amanda was called away and Faith tried to focus on something, anything that wasn't Dylan. Luckily, several people stopped to comment on her arrangements, so that gave her a ready-made distraction.

By the time the photographer said she had enough shots and called a halt, Faith had successfully avoided looking at Dylan since he'd asked her if she was okay. So when he appeared in front of her, tall, dark and smiling, she lost her breath.

"You ready to go?" he asked.

She blinked. "Yeah. You sure you don't mind dropping me home? I can catch a cab."

"Actually, I was thinking we should do something to celebrate the success of your designs first."

"Like what?" she practically stammered. *Celebration* and *Dylan* were two words that could be dangerous when paired together.

He ran a hand over his jaw. "A fine champagne should do it."

She looked around. "Here?" Maybe it wouldn't be so dangerous if the others were involved as well.

"I need to drop these flowers off at my place so the delivery van can be picked up—the iris is still under wraps, so I can't let them go anywhere else. But there's a bar downstairs in my building. How about we drive over, I'll race the arrangements upstairs and then we can have a bottle of their best champagne in the bar before I drop you home?"

The plan sounded harmless—he hadn't suggested she go up to his apartment with him, so they'd be surrounded by people the whole time. They couldn't get carried away the way they had at the store on their first meeting. And truth was, she was too buzzed about the day's events to go home just yet. This would be the perfect way to end the day: a small celebration with the person who understood how much making those arrangements and having them photographed for the publicity posters meant to her.

"I'd love to," she said.

They set the flowers back in the boxes and carried them out to the delivery van, said their farewells and set off for Dylan's building. Once they got there and parked, he went around to the back of the van and opened the doors.

"How about you grab us a table while I take these up," he said as he drew out the boxes. "I'll only be a couple of minutes."

"Sure," she said. Part of her wanted to go with him and see his apartment, and the other part knew how dangerous that would be. Best to stay to public areas.

It was still fairly early, and the bar mainly had the after-work crowd, not the evening revelers yet, so she didn't have any trouble finding a booth. She was perusing the cocktail list on the wall behind her when she heard the sound of fabric moving over vinyl. Dylan slid onto the bench seat across from her. His sculpted cheekbones and sparkling green eyes seemed to make the whole world brighter.

"Would you prefer a cocktail?" he asked.

It wouldn't be very smart to drink stronger alcohol when she was alone with this man. "No, I think you're right. Champagne is perfect to celebrate."

"Good, because I just ordered a bottle." His grin just about had her melting on the spot. And over the course of a couple of glasses of champagne each, the effect of Dylan Hawke on her system only intensified.

His cell beeped and he fished it from his pocket. "That was quick," he said as he thumbed some buttons. "The photographer has sent some preliminary shots over."

Her pulse jumped. "Can I see?"

He turned the cell screen to her, but the images were small, so she couldn't see much detail on how the individual iris looked at the center of the shot. "I can't tell much," she said.

He turned the cell back to himself and rotated it as he swiped the screen, flicking through the photos. "We could run up to my apartment and look at them on my computer screen."

He'd made the suggestion almost absent-mindedly, not lifting his gaze from the photos on his phone, and she wondered if he realized the enormity of the possible consequences of his offer.

"Is that wise?" she asked and laced her hands together in her lap. "We agreed it was best to stick to public places."

He stilled. Then his gaze slowly lifted to meet hers. She was right—he hadn't thought it through. He blew out a breath and shrugged. "It'll be fine. It would only be a few minutes, and we'll be focused on the flowers. Then I'll bring you straight back down and drop you home."

She chewed on her bottom lip. She really did want to see those photos, and since the flower was a secret, she wouldn't ask him to forward them to her own email address, so this was the only chance she'd have to get a sneak peek before the posters were produced. Surely she could control her reaction to this man for a few minutes. In fact, when she thought of it that way, her caution seemed crazy—she wasn't ruled by her lusts. Of course she could keep her hands to herself.

Decision made, she nodded. "I'd appreciate that."

She followed him out of the bar, then down a short corridor to a bank of elevators. One was waiting and he ushered her inside, then punched in a code before hitting the *P* button, which she assumed stood for *penthouse*.

They were silent as they stood side by side in the small space, both watching the doors. Perhaps this had been a bad idea after all. Even these first few moments of being alone were filled with tension. A feeling of leashed anticipation.

She opened her mouth to suggest they skip this and he drop her home when the doors whooshed open. He held out a hand to let her precede him into another hallway, and she hesitated.

"Is something wrong?" he asked.

Her mouth was suddenly dry, so she swallowed before speaking. "I guess I'm having second thoughts."

"You know," he said, reaching out to hold the lift doors, "we've been alone quite a bit of time, if you think about it. In the car, the delivery van, the room where you've been working at Liam's. And not once in those times did I lose control and leap on you."

But each of those times there had been the threat of someone entering the room or people in other cars looking through the windows. This time they'd be utterly alone. She moistened her lips.

"If it helps," he said, one corner of his mouth turning up, "I swear to keep my hands to myself."

She believed him. In the time she'd known him, he'd proved to be a man of his word. So she nodded, but as he unlocked his door, she admitted to herself that it wasn't *his* control she was worried about...

Dylan pushed open his door and hoped like hell he could keep the promise he'd just made.

"Do you want anything? A drink? Water?"

She shook her head. He closed the door behind her, then led the way through his living room to a study off to the side. As he booted up the computer, he pulled a second chair over to the desk, but Faith was still in the doorway, standing at an angle, looking out into his living room. He moved to her side, curious to see what she was looking at. Following her line of vision, his gaze landed on the flower arrangements she'd made only hours before.

"You did a really good job," he said, his voice low. "They're beautiful."

She didn't move. "Mainly due to Liam's work creating the Ruby Iris."

"No, mainly due to you. You forget what line of work I'm in." With a gentle finger, he turned her chin to him so he could see her eyes. So she could see his and know he meant this. "I've seen beautiful flowers rendered awkward by a bad arrangement. You, however, have enhanced the Ruby Iris's beauty."

Her eyes darkened. He realized she was close enough that he could lean in and kiss her again. Hell, how he wanted to. But he'd made her a promise to keep his hands to himself. So he dropped his hand and stepped back.

He cleared his throat to get his voice to work again.

"Speaking of your skill, let's have a look at those photos."

He held a chair out for her, then sat in his and opened the email.

There was a tiny gasp from beside him, and he turned to watch her reaction. "What do you think?" he asked.

"I've taken snapshots of my arrangements before, but I've never seen professional photos of them." Her voice was soft, as if she wasn't even conscious she was speaking.

"The photographer has done a good job." He passed the mouse to her so she could flick through the photos at her own pace.

"The lighting is amazing," she said as she scrolled. "And the angles…"

He was sure the lighting and angles were out of this world, but he didn't even glimpse them. His attention was firmly focused on Faith. Her eyes shone with unshed tears—were they of pride? Or joy? As one of those tears broke away and made a track down her cheek, he brushed it away with his thumb.

She turned to him, eyes shocked, lips slightly parted. "Dylan—"

He withdrew his hand and sat on it and his other hand for good measure. "I'm sorry. I promised not to touch you, and I won't."

Her chest rose and fell more quickly than it had only a few minutes before. "You cross your heart?"

"Yes. I give you my word."

She sucked her luscious bottom lip into her mouth, obviously considering something. Finally she released her lip and met his gaze again. "Then do you mind if I do something?"

"Whatever you want," he said and meant it.

She lifted her hand and cupped the side of his face, running her thumb along his skin, the roughness of his jaw. "I've been dreaming about doing this, but I knew if I did, it would start something neither of us wanted. But since you've promised, then I just wanted to see…"

His pulse had spiked at her touch, and now it raced even faster.

"Faith," he said, his voice ragged. "Have a little mercy."

"Just a moment more," she whispered as her other hand joined in the exploration of his face.

Dylan tensed the muscles in his arms, trying to retain control over them, but he kept sitting on his hands. He didn't dare move. Then her index finger brushed over his lips, and he couldn't stop his tongue darting out to meet it. She pressed a little harder into his bottom lip, and he caught the tip of her finger between his teeth. She moistened her own lips and watched his mouth as if there was nothing she wanted more than to kiss him. He knew exactly how that felt.

"Faith," he said as her fingers moved to his throat. "This is a dangerous game."

"I'll stop in a moment." But her fingers continued their path, moving from his throat up to thread through his hair. "I've been thinking, daydreaming about doing this, and I'll never get another chance."

He groaned. She'd been daydreaming about him? About touching him?

All the blood in his body headed south. He adjusted his position on the chair but didn't release his hands.

"It seems as if it's been forever since our kiss," she continued as her hands traced a path down his throat again, but this time not stopping, instead spreading over his chest. "And even though this can't go anywhere, I've sometimes thought I'd die if I never touched you again. So I just want to make a memory to keep."

"You'll be the death of me." His head dropped back—he couldn't handle her touch combined with the sight of her a moment longer. Though some devil inside him made him ask, "Tell me what else you daydreamed."

There was a pause and he thought she wasn't going to answer, until in a soft voice she said, "You were touching me as well."

"I've thought about that." A lot. And he was thinking about it now. There was something about this woman who made him feel more alive than he had in a long time. Being around her when she worked, laughing with her, having her hands on him.

"Dylan?" she whispered, her voice close to his ear.

Her breath was warm on his earlobe, and he could barely get enough brain cells working to answer. "Yes?"

"What would it take to get you to break that promise?"

A shudder raced through his body. "Faith," he warned.

"Would you touch me if I begged?" Her hands trailed down his arms to rest on his wrists—as far as she could go while he was still sitting on his hands.

His arms trembled but he didn't move, couldn't speak. Then her hands cupped either side of his face and brought his gaze down to land on her. The air from her lungs fanned across his face.

"Please," she whispered against his lips, and then leaned in the last inch and kissed him.

And his last thread of control snapped.

# Seven

Faith knew she was being reckless, but the moment Dylan's mouth closed the tiny space to reach hers, she didn't care. She'd been craving this since the last time they'd kissed. Had been craving *him*.

As she gently landed in his lap, his tongue pushed between her parted lips. She couldn't have contained the sound of satisfaction that rose in her throat if she'd tried. And she definitely didn't want to try. She could talk for an hour about the reasons they shouldn't cross the line again, but this, *this* felt too right. She speared her hands through his hair, reveling in the slide of it over her sensitive fingers.

His arms closed around her, holding her close, but it wasn't close enough. She dug at his waistband until she worked his shirt free, then skimmed her hands underneath, over his abdomen and up as high as she could reach with the fabric restraining her hands. His light chest hair tickled, and she dug her nails in.

"Faith," he said as his head dropped back, but his arms didn't relax their grip an inch.

His arousal pressed against the underside of her thighs, and she wriggled against it. A groan seemed to be ripped from him, and he lifted his head to meet her eyes. "I knew you'd be the death of me."

She smiled and kissed him. He tasted of champagne and heat, and she'd never tasted anything so decadent. After minutes, or hours, her lungs screamed for air, so she pulled back, gasping, but he didn't miss a beat. He scraped his teeth across her earlobe, and electric shivers radiated out across her body. She'd never been this desperate for any man. There was something about Dylan Hawke that drove her to the brink of insanity.

"If we're doing this—" he said, gasping between words.

Before he could finish his sentence, she said, "Oh, we're doing this."

He grinned against her mouth. "Then let's move somewhere more comfortable."

He stood, taking her with him and setting her on her feet, and began to walk her backward, through the living room and down the hall, expertly guiding her so that she didn't hit anything, his mouth not leaving hers the entire time.

Once they reached his bedroom, she had no interest in looking around except to ensure there was a bed. Her gaze found a large one with a dark wood headboard and a navy blue comforter and pillows. Perfect. Dylan flicked on a lamp, and its soft yellow light joined the last rays of the sunset filtering through large windows that overlooked downtown LA. The sunset was stunning, but nothing compared with the man before her.

His hands explored her shape through her clothes, but she had less patience—she slid her hands under his cotton shirt so that she could feel his skin again. It had been only minutes since she'd touched his bare chest, but she missed the sensation. She worked up from the ridges of his abdomen, higher, until she found the crisp hair that covered his pecs. It still wasn't enough, so she unbuttoned the shirt and began the journey again, this time with more freedom.

He groaned and pulled her closer, trapping her hands between them, and with palms cupping her bottom, he lifted her until she was standing on her toes, pressed against him. The ridge of his arousal pressed at the juncture of her thighs, the pressure only teasing and nowhere near enough. There was an ache deep inside her and it was only intensifying.

With a hand flat on his chest, she pushed him back. She reached out and unbuckled his belt, pulling it through the loopholes until it came free in her hands, and then dropped it over her shoulder. It clattered on the polished wood floor, and Dylan let out a laugh.

"Seems like you have flair in more than one area of your life, Faith Sixty-Three."

"Seems like you're a smooth talker in more than one area of your life." She undid the button at the top of his trousers and slowly lowered the zipper. With thumbs tucked into the sides, he gave the trousers a nudge and they fell to his ankles, along with his underwear.

He continued to walk her backward to the bed, but she put her hands on his shoulders, stilling him. "Give me a moment to appreciate you."

Obligingly he nodded, but almost immediately he cradled her face and kissed her again. She moved in, closing the distance between them, feeling the heat of his naked body through his clothes. So much, but not enough.

When she didn't think she could take it another second, he stepped backward until he hit the side of the bed and then sank down, bringing her with him to straddle his lap. She pushed up on her knees to give herself a little extra height and took control of the kiss. He ran his hands along her exposed thighs, up underneath her skirt, and then wrapped them around her hips. Her heart beat so strongly, she could feel the resonant thud through her entire body.

"Dylan," she breathed between kisses. She'd never wanted a man this badly before. Couldn't imagine ever wanting someone this badly again.

One by one, he undid the buttons on her blouse, and then peeled the fabric back to reveal her blush-pink demicup bra. He traced a finger around its lacy edges and over the slope of her breasts just before they disappeared into the cups. "So beautiful," he breathed. "Every inch of you is just so beautiful, Faith."

He hooked a finger into one of the cups, pushing down, seeking, and ran the back of his nail over her nipple. She shuddered. The corner of his mouth quirked up, and he did it again, eliciting the same response. Then he pulled the lace down, exposing her breast, and her back arched.

His mouth closed over her nipple and she shuddered. He wrapped an arm around her back, holding her to him as his teeth scraped her skin, followed by his tongue licking her. Through the fog of desire, she was only barely aware of his free hand working deftly behind her to undo the catch on her bra. He finally pulled it down her arms and threw it to the side.

The knowledge that they wouldn't have to stop before they were carried away this time created an intimacy that stole her breath. After all the wanting, finally being together without the barriers between their skin was almost too much to comprehend.

She pushed his open shirt over his shoulders, kissing the skin she'd exposed. The muscles of his shoulders bunched and tensed as first her lips made contact, then her tongue. The scent of his skin was intoxicating.

He fell back against the covers, taking her with him. She was still straddling his hips but now leaning her weight against his torso. She had a semblance of control, but her options for touching him were limited because most of him was either covered by her or hidden against the comforter. He, however, had full access and was taking most delicious advantage, his hands exploring her back, her sides, wherever he could reach.

Her skin was scorching, everything inside her so hot she thought she might explode into flames. And if that happened, so be it—being with Dylan would be more than worth it.

Then he rolled them over so that she was beneath him, his glorious weight pushing her into the mattress. But before she'd had a chance to appreciate the sensation fully, he moved down the bed, lifting her knee as he went. He ran his lips along the inside of her calf, stopping to press a kiss and then to bite lightly at the sensitive back of her knee. Electricity shot along her veins. His hands moved higher, capturing her skirt as he went, taking the fabric with him as his fingers skimmed over her thighs, her hips, until it bunched at her waist.

His fingers hooked under the sides of her pale pink underwear, pulling it inch by inch down her legs. Once it was removed, he covered her with one hand, applying delicious pressure, moving in patterns that were designed to take her to the brink.

Without pausing his hand, he moved back up her body to find her gaze and placed a tender, lingering kiss on her lips. "I feel as if I've wanted you forever. I can't believe you're really here."

"I can barely believe I'm here, either." Her heart squeezed tight at his expression. "It's like a dream."

"It's no dream," he said with a wicked grin. "Let me show you how real this is."

Breaking contact, he disappeared for excruciating moments before reappearing with a foil packet. He ripped it open, but before he could put the condom on, she took it from him and rolled it down his length. When it was on, she circled him with her hand and, taking her time, let herself learn his shape, his secrets. Air hissed out from between his teeth.

Abruptly, and with a pained expression on his face, he grabbed her wrists, freed himself and knelt between her legs. As he lifted her hips, she held her breath. Then he guided himself to her and filled her bit by bit until she gasped.

"Okay?" he asked, his brow furrowed.

She smiled. "More than okay."

He returned the smile and then began to move. She met each stroke, wanting to make the most of every last sensation. But as the tension inside her climbed, she forgot to move, forgot everything but Dylan above her.

His rhythm was driving her slowly out of her mind. She gripped frantically at his back, trying to find purchase, but it felt as if the world was slipping away and all that remained was Dylan moving above her, within her.

Heated breaths near her ear drove her higher, his whispered words telling her she was beautiful, higher still.

His hand snaked down to where their bodies joined, and as he applied pressure with his thumb, she called out his name and exploded into a thousand little pieces, every single one of them filled with bright, shining light. He groaned, and a few strokes later he followed her over the edge before slumping his weight on top of her. She welcomed the heaviness as if it could keep her grounded here on Earth while her soul wanted to fly away.

Whispering her name, Dylan rolled to the side, taking her with him, holding her close. She nestled against his chest, feeling more safe and secure than she could ever remember.

Faith woke slowly and stretched, deep contentment filling her body, down to her bones. And before she was even fully awake, she was wary. It was the contentment that made her suspicious—she'd learned young not to trust the feeling.

The night before came back to her in snatches, then in its entirety. The sensation of Dylan's hand caressing her face, the taste of him in her mouth, the sound he'd made at the back of his throat when he'd found his release.

She'd made love with Dylan, and it had been glorious. And dangerous.

High moments had always preceded her lowest moments, and last night had been a huge high, meaning there was a low—just as huge—coming, whether she was ready or not.

She opened her groggy eyes to the early morning light and found Dylan lying a hand span away on the thick white sheets, watching her. No chance of sneaking away or not facing the consequences of what they'd done.

"Good morning," he said. His voice was sleep-roughened and his hair rumpled, but his expression was guarded. She couldn't get a read on him.

"Good morning," she replied and gathered the sheet a little higher to reach her neck, as if that could give her a buffer between what they'd shared last night and the reality of the morning after. They'd gone too far this time and crossed a line that couldn't be uncrossed. She'd slept with the boss.

He arched an eyebrow and looked pointedly at the sheet she was clutching. "It's a little late for that, don't you think?"

Memories assaulted her—of seducing him, of begging him to touch her. Even as her skin heated with desire, she recognized that this mess they were in was her fault, and she had to find a way to fix it.

"Dylan—" she began, gripping the sheet more firmly.

Before she could say anything else, he interrupted with a false smile stretched across his face. "I'll make us some coffee."

He swung his legs out from the bed, the sheet dropping away to reveal six feet of toned perfection. Her breath caught high in her throat. Dylan in the early morning light was just as impressive as Dylan in the lamplight in the middle of the night. Her hand demanded a chance to touch, but that was what had gotten her into this situation in the first place, so she resisted. Barely.

He found a pair of jeans in his closet, slipped them on and then pulled a charcoal T-shirt over his head before turning back to her.

He indicated a door to the left that she remembered from last night was the bathroom. "Feel free to use the shower or whatever you need."

"Thanks," she said, not releasing the sheet even an inch. She would have loved a shower, but more than that, she wanted to be home, safe and cocooned. Away from temptation that could ruin everything and these messy feelings that Dylan seemed to evoke in her.

After he left the room, she jumped up and grabbed her clothes from the floor where he'd dropped them after he peeled them off her. Maybe once she was dressed she'd feel more in control, though she had a sneaking suspicion it wouldn't be enough.

She'd been becoming more concerned about her attachment to this man every time she saw him. But in her experience, attachments didn't last. Her family had shown her that no matter how sincere people appeared, they'd drop you like a hotcake when someone better came along. And Dylan had had a reputation as a playboy before they met.

Her aunt had promised that she loved her and would always be there for her, but as soon as she'd gotten pregnant, she'd shipped the eleven-year-old Faith off to her grandparents.

Her aunt had been apologetic, saying she just didn't think she could cope with a new baby as well as a child in the house, and Faith had understood that. She'd never blamed her aunt. Instead, she'd just felt stupid that she'd let herself believe this time it might be different. Had let herself hope.

Hope was dangerous.

After the way she'd felt in his arms last night, it was clear that if she let herself begin to hope with Dylan, it would end up devastating her when he left. She'd allowed herself to feel too much.

By reputation, Dylan Hawke was the last man whose commitment she could depend on. No matter how sweet he was being to her now, she'd never be able to hold his attention for long. Better they step back from each other now, before she was hurt by his straying attention later.

As she found her way down the hallway to the kitchen, the scent of freshly brewed coffee hit her senses, promising that everything would be better after she was caffeinated.

She rounded the corner and found Dylan leaning back against the counter, tapping his fingers in a rapid tattoo. He looked about as confused as she felt, and that gave her the confidence she needed.

"I think we need to talk," she said, hoping her voice didn't wobble.

Dylan nodded and handed her a mug of coffee. "I'm sorry about last night."

"If anyone's going to apologize, it should be me." She looked down into her steaming mug. "You held to your word longer than I did."

"Nevertheless, I shouldn't have given in at all." He rubbed a hand up and down his face, clearly annoyed at himself.

"Dylan, I don't want to get into the blame game. I'd rather we look at where we go from here." She leaned a hip on the counter across from him. "First, I think we crossed a line."

He coughed, almost choking on his coffee. "That's pretty safe to say."

At least they agreed on that. However, what to do about it was another matter entirely. She prayed for the strength to see this through. To avoid giving in and dragging him back to the bedroom now.

Interlacing her fingers in her lap, she focused on the cabinet over his shoulder as she spoke. "Crossing lines is becoming something of a habit for us."

"A habit?" He coughed out a laugh. "More like an addiction."

"And like all addictions, it's not healthy," she said reluctantly. "But clearly, I don't know how to stop."

He gave her a wry smile. "I guess that's the exact reason why people struggle with addictions. The how to stop part is hard."

Taking a deep breath, she met his gaze squarely. "So what do you think we should do?"

"There's only one solution. Cold turkey." There was a slight wince in his features as he said the words.

"That sounds final." And severe. Her body tensed just thinking about it. She imagined her reaction the next time she saw him, having to lock down her need as if they hadn't shared the deepest of connections. "How would cold turkey work?"

He put his empty mug in the sink and was silent for a long moment, his gaze trained on the view out the window. When he spoke again, he didn't turn back. "You're still working on the project, so we'll be seeing each other at meetings and at Liam's lab. But in general, we give up spending time alone."

"We haven't gone out of our way to spend time alone up until now. It's just kind of happened." When said aloud, it sounded feeble, but since that first night, when she'd realized they had a problem, they'd both tried to be careful. Yet they'd still ended up in his bed.

He turned back to her, crossing his arms over his chest, a tiny frown line appearing between his eyebrows. "New rules, new level of caution. I'll stay away from the Santa Monica store. If the opportunity arises to, say, attend a photo shoot together, one of us declines."

She nodded slowly. "We become extravigilant."

"Exactly." But he didn't meet her eyes as he said it.

It seemed surreal to be talking about this, to be more attracted to someone than she'd ever been but discussing ways to not act on it. Though it was the strength of that attraction that was the exact problem.

Hope was dangerous.

"So," she said, seeking to disarm some of the tension that had grown between them in the last ten minutes, "I guess standing around in your kitchen early in the morning is probably not something we should be doing, either."

"Nope," he said, his lips curving in a tight smile. "Especially with the way my thoughts are heading, seeing you leaning against my cabinetry."

She stepped away from the counter, which only brought her closer to him. In two steps, she could be in his arms again…

She bit down on her lip. He was right—there was no safe way to spend time alone together.

"Okay," she said, feeling as if she was signing her own death warrant. But she wouldn't give up this job or the opportunities Hawke's Blooms could offer her at this stage in her career. And if she wanted the job, she couldn't sleep with the boss. "I agree to your new plan."

He held out a hand for her mug, and as she gave it to him, his hand closed around hers for a long moment. "Even though we're trying to avoid repeating it, I want you to know I've enjoyed every moment I've spent with you, Faith Sixty-Three."

A ball of emotion rose up and lodged itself in her throat, and she had to swallow to get her voice to work. "I've enjoyed the time I've spent with you, too."

"Come on," he said, his voice rough. "I'll drive you out to get your car."

He grabbed his keys from the end of the counter, and she followed him out, stopping only to pick up her handbag and, one last time, to look around the apartment where she'd glimpsed heaven.

# Eight

Dylan knocked on the door of Faith's ground-floor apartment and stepped back to wait. It had been almost a month since the night she'd stayed at his place. The night that had rocked him to his core. In that time, they'd seen each other at Liam's research lab and in meetings about the launch, but, as agreed, they hadn't spent any time alone together. And every day it had been a little more difficult than the day before to keep himself from calling her.

But that third date had been weighing on his mind. It was a loose end that needed clearing up, and it was time he did just that. The closure would help him move forward. Maybe he was grasping at straws, but nothing else had worked so far to help him forget her and move on.

The apartment door opened to reveal Faith in shorts and a T-shirt, her face makeup-free and her curling hair loose around her shoulders. She stole his breath.

"Dylan," she said, her voice betraying her surprise.

"Sorry for the unannounced visit." He smiled and dug his hands into his pockets. "Do you mind if I come in for a couple of minutes?"

She blinked and then opened the door wider. "Sure."

Once inside, he turned to take in the decor. Or lack of decor. The place was beyond minimalist—it was practically bare. There was an old sofa, a coffee table and a TV. The coffee table had a small pile of floristry magazines sitting haphazardly on it, and an empty mug. No bright cushions on the sofa, no colorful paintings on the walls. No collections of eccentric odds and ends, no surprises at all. It was like the anti-Faith apartment.

There was a kitchen beside the living room, with a counter acting as a divider between the rooms. Except for a chrome toaster and a mismatched wooden knife block, the kitchen counters were bare, echoing the interior design of the living room. He'd expected flair. Color. Personality. Faith.

"Can I get you a drink?" she asked, her features schooled to blank.

He shook his head and brought his attention back to the reason he'd come. "No, I won't be here long."

"Even so, maybe we should have this conversation outside." She headed out through the door she'd opened for him and stood in the small courtyard at the front of the apartment block. There were a few dry-looking shrubs enclosing a paved square that was heavily shaded by the building, and it looked about as wrong for her as the interior did.

"Is there a problem with the launch?" she asked, crossing her arms under her breasts.

The launch was only a week away and plans were

in full swing, but it was running as smoothly as could be expected. But it was connected to why he'd knocked on her door this morning.

He cleared his throat. "We need to talk about the auction and our last date."

He'd wanted to bring it up again for a while now, but it didn't seem right to talk about it when they were at work. Where he was the boss and she was his employee. Those roles didn't disappear simply by talking to her here, obviously, but at least by discussing the situation when they were on her turf, it felt a little more equal.

She snapped off a leaf from a nearby shrub and crumpled it in her fingers. "I've told you we can let that slide. I've already got more than I expected from the auction with this assignment working with the Ruby Iris."

That sounded fine in theory, but he needed the closure, so he ignored her objection. "And I've told you that I won't let it slide. You paid to have me look more closely at your floristry skills and I did, but I want to make sure you've had the opportunity to say all you need to about where you see yourself in the company." He offered her a smile. "Since we're both going to the launch anyway, I thought we could go together and it could serve as our final date."

She shifted her weight from one leg to the other. "I seem to remember we decided to keep our distance. To go cold turkey. In fact, those rules pretty much exclude you even being here today."

"It's been almost a month without incident. I think we're fine." Well, *she* seemed fine, anyway. He was still kept awake at night, replaying memories of their night together. Of the feel of her skin, the touch of her lips as she kissed him in desperation.

She, however, seemed unaffected, which was more than a little annoying.

"So how would you see this working?" she asked, sounding unconvinced.

"I'll pick you up, like a date. We've never had any problems being alone in a car together, so that should be fine. Then we'll attend the launch together. Perhaps dance, but since we'll be in public, surrounded by Hawke's Blooms staff and management, there won't be any chance to get carried away. Then I'll drop you home."

"That last point sounds like a danger area," she said as she ran her hands over a branch near her shoulder.

"Good point." In theory, it would only be the same level of temptation that they had right now, but on the night of the launch, they'd both be wearing their finest, would have danced, perhaps would have had a glass or two of champagne. "I'll arrange a limo to drop you home. It will be on standby so you can leave when you want to. Alone."

She screwed up her nose as she considered. "Okay, that sounds harmless enough. And then we'll be square?"

"Then we'll be square," he confirmed. Of course, he was going to reimburse her the money she'd paid for the dates as soon as they'd had the last one, despite her earlier protests. Eight thousand two hundred dollars was a lot of money for someone on her wage.

And speaking of money, there was one other aspect of this last date that needed addressing. "Also, I'd appreciate it if you'd let me buy you a dress for the launch."

She shook her head. "You don't have to buy me a dress, Dylan."

He'd expected opposition, so it didn't faze him. He rocked back on his heels and laid out his reasoning. "You admitted that you spent almost all your savings at the auction, so yes, I do. Will it help if I promise not to buy you a corsage?"

"Dylan—" she began, but he interrupted.

"Humor me. Let me buy you a dress, we'll have the date, and then we can properly go back to being a boss and an employee."

"You want to take me shopping?" She arched an eyebrow. "Alone?"

Alone would be crazy. Luckily, he'd already come up with a solution. "I've arranged a personal shopper who will take us to a store after closing time. We'll not only have private access to the store and advice but also be chaperoned."

She didn't say anything, but he wanted this closure, so he smiled and said, "Just say yes, Faith."

She blew out a breath. "Okay, sure."

Good. Part of him was glad he'd been able to get her to agree. After this he'd be able to move on. Another part of him was wondering if he'd stepped out of the frying pan into the fire.

Faith pulled up in the parking lot of the upscale clothing store and let out a sigh. She was looking forward to spending time with Dylan far more than she should, and that worried her.

Pretending to be unaffected by him in her apartment had almost cost her her sanity. If he hadn't promised to have a personal shopper here tonight, she would never have agreed. Though he'd seemed remarkably unaffected when he'd made the offer, which was hardly fair. If she was struggling, then it would boost her ego if he'd been struggling right along with her.

Perhaps he'd moved on already? Her stomach dipped at the thought, but it would be for the best. Yes, indeed. It was exactly what they needed to happen. If only it didn't feel like the end of the world to contemplate…

His Porsche pulled up beside her. Dylan stepped out and paused to set the keyless lock. He wore jeans and a white polo shirt—it was the only time she'd seen him in jeans besides the morning after they'd made love. She gripped the steering wheel tighter. The memory threatened to overwhelm her with sensation, so she pushed it to the back of her mind and focused on the here and now. However, the fact that the here and now consisted of Dylan's rear end outlined by soft denim wasn't helping her gain control much.

"Evening, Faith," he said as he opened her car door. The deep, sexy drawl sent a shiver up her spine. She stepped out and Dylan closed the door.

"Hello, Dylan," she said. Then, before she could give herself away, she smiled and locked her car. "Is the personal shopper here already or do we need to wait?"

"She's inside."

"Let's not keep her waiting, then," she said and set off for the entrance.

Dylan was beside her in two strides. "You know, you seem a lot more keen about this than I expected."

Actually, she was keen to have another person in the mix and avoid being alone with him, especially in a dimly lit parking lot. If he'd moved on, she wasn't letting him know she was still back where she'd been the night they'd made love. She straightened her spine.

"The sooner we start, the sooner it will be over," she said over her shoulder.

A middle-aged woman wearing a designer pantsuit, her hair in a sleek silver bob, opened the door for them. "Dylan and Faith?" she asked.

"That's us," Dylan said, holding out his hand.

"I'm Julie." She shook Dylan's hand and then held her hand out to Faith. "As I understand it, we're looking for an outfit for Faith to wear to an event?"

"Yes," Faith said. "So, something formal."

"Lovely. The formal section is this way." She moved away, and Faith turned to Dylan.

"You don't need to hang around," she said brightly. "Or if you want to stay, you could wait over by the doors? You'll get bored looking at women's clothes." The last thing she wanted was to be trying on clothes with him within touching distance.

He grinned. "Not a chance. I'm staying to make sure you don't weasel out."

"What if I promise—"

Dylan cut her off. "I'm staying, Faith, so you may as well catch up with Julie."

"Sure," she said on a sigh. She'd come to learn a thing or two about this man, and she could tell this wasn't a battle she was going to win. She followed the path Julie had taken to the formal wear section, very aware of Dylan's gaze on her as he tagged along.

Once they arrived, Julie made a sweeping gesture with her arm to point out the options. "Did you have anything in mind? Some guidelines so I know where to start?"

Faith chewed the inside of her cheek, trying to come up with some ideas. She'd been too worried about being here with Dylan to think about the actual dress.

"Something bright," Dylan said. "Vibrant."

"Okay, good." Julie nodded. "Anything else?"

Dylan rocked back on his heels. "Perhaps something quirky. She looks great in halter necks, but then, she looks great in everything, so that shouldn't limit you."

Faith watched the exchange, a little stunned. Dylan glanced over and caught her expression. "What? I've been paying attention."

He certainly had. Suddenly this situation they were in tonight felt even more uneven than it had earlier. She lifted her chin. "So what are you planning on wearing to the launch?"

He shrugged. "A suit, I guess."

"White shirt and a random tie from your closet?" she asked sweetly.

"Probably."

She shook her head in mock disappointment. "Conservative choice."

One corner of his mouth twitched. "Is that so?"

"New deal." She planted her hands on her hips. "You get to stay and have input into what I wear if I can choose something for you to wear."

He blinked slowly. "You're changing the rules?"

"I am." She stood a little taller. "You got a problem with that?"

"Nope. I've always liked your attitude. Deal." He turned to Julie. "We'll need time in the menswear section as well."

They walked around both sections of the store for twenty minutes, each handing garments to Julie to take to the other's changing room. By the time they were finished, there were probably more clothes in there waiting for them than left on the shelves.

"We're done," Dylan said.

Julie nodded. "Okay, follow me."

She led them into a room the size of a small store in itself. It was circular, with mirrored doors along the outer wall and a round sofa in the middle. On one side of the room was a long chrome stand on wheels that was full of the dresses Faith had agreed to try on, and on the other side of the room was a matching stand with the clothes for Dylan. There was also an ice bucket on a stand, with champagne chilling.

Julie lifted the bottle. "How about we start with a glass of bubbly?"

Faith glanced at Dylan, and he raised an eyebrow, leaving it to her. The night they'd lost control had started with champagne… But tonight they were chaperoned, and she was having fun, so the champagne would be nice.

She nodded at Julie. "Thank you."

Julie poured two glasses and handed them over. Dylan clinked his to Faith's. "Here's to an interesting night."

"Cheers," she said and took a sip before handing her glass back to Julie and heading for her changing room. There were so many dresses, she didn't know where to start, so she grabbed the first one her hand landed on and slipped through the door.

It was an electric-blue velvet, floor-length number. As she was zipping up, Julie called out, "How's it going? Need any help?"

"I'm fine, thanks. The zip is on the side."

She adjusted the dress and looked in the mirror. The color was amazing on her, and the dress itself made her look more elegant than she'd anticipated. As she opened the door, Dylan stilled, his hand freezing on the shirt cuff he'd been adjusting.

He cleared his throat. "Stunning. But it's not the right one."

Faith looked down at the dress. "I like it."

"I like it, too. But it's not the right one."

She was about to argue when she caught sight of the rack full of dresses still to try. No point becoming attached to the first one, anyway. "Turn around and show me what you're wearing."

He held his arms out and turned, letting her see. He'd chosen the most conservative of all the options—a cream shirt with a black suit and charcoal tie. The colors set off his tan, but she smiled and said, "I like it, but it's not the right one."

Julie jumped up from the sofa. "Good, we're narrowing it down. Next! I'll take those two outfits back into the store when you have them off."

Faith grabbed another dress and slipped back into the changing room. For the next five changes, Dylan's eyes heated with approval, but he said each wasn't the right one, so she kept going, wondering what he was waiting for.

And for each of those five changes, she'd also rejected his outfits. Seeing him in a fitted white shirt that accentuated the breadth of his shoulders and his toned biceps had made her mouth dry, but she was waiting for something a little bit different.

She emerged wearing the sixth dress, a light-as-air

confection in mint green that shimmered like mother-of-pearl and seemed to float and sparkle as she moved.

Dylan's eyes darkened when he saw her. "Now we're getting somewhere." He reached out to touch the sleeve, and the warmth of his hand seeped through the light fabric. "This is more how I see you."

"What do you mean?" she asked, looking down at the dress.

"Let me ask you a question instead." He lifted her chin with a crooked finger. "I've seen your heart. When you make flower arrangements, your heart is on display. Crab apple and mint, the Ruby Iris with pale pink blooms and crystals. You're unique, you're creative and you're effervescent. So why is your apartment so plain that it's practically military issue?"

She moved away, giving herself a moment to think. They'd agreed not to spend time alone together, so where did that leave soul-baring admissions? Maybe it would be best not to get too deep for exactly the same reasons.

She shrugged. "I just haven't gotten around to decorating yet. It doesn't seem as if I've been there long enough."

"It's more than that," he said, moving back into her field of vision. "It's part of not wanting to put down roots, isn't it? Being a rolling stone?"

This man saw through her far too easily. She let out a long breath and told him more than she'd ever told a living soul. "There was one time when I was nine. I was living with my grandparents, and I'd thought I was finally settled, that I'd finish growing up at their house." She'd begun to hope. "I looked through magazines and ripped out posters of bands and actors that my little nine-year-old heart was crushing on, and I covered my walls with them. It was more than just putting posters up. It was about marking my territory. That room was mine, you know?"

"Yeah, I do," he said softly, his green eyes intense.

"I spent ridiculous amounts of time arranging who to put where and who could be side by side with someone else. I was so proud of that damn wall when I was finished that I would lie on my bed and just stare at it."

He ran a hand up and down her back, hypnotizing her into a sense of calm. "What happened to the wall, Faith?"

"Nothing. The wall was fine." She swallowed hard. "But my father called one night and said he was picking me up in the morning to take me out to a theme park. Once we were on the road, he told me he was dropping me off with my mother afterward. She wanted to give parenthood another go."

Dylan's body tensed, but his voice remained even. "What about your things?"

"My grandparents had packed my clothes while I was having breakfast—I didn't have a lot—and they were already in the back of the truck." The betrayal of their not giving her advance warning, of always keeping her in the dark, still stung. "Part of me was happy my mother wanted me, but part of me was thinking about my wall. About where I'd begun to feel settled."

"Oh, baby," he said on a sigh. "You had it all ripped out from under you again."

"I never put anything up on a wall again. And the next time I went back to my grandparents' to live— after my aunt handed me back when I was eleven— I ripped down every one of those pictures and threw them in the trash." She rubbed at her breastbone. That damn memory still had the power to hurt, even after all these years.

"Hey, come here," he said, and wrapped his arms around her.

She just stood in his embrace, not relaxing. "I'm okay."

"I know you are," he said gently. "But I'm going to hug you anyway."

It was the perfect thing to say, and she let herself lean against his solid chest to soak up his strength for just a moment. Then she chuckled—of course it was the perfect thing to say, since he was a known charmer.

He dipped his head. "What's funny?"

"You know, I was warned about your way with words," she said, biting down on a smile and stepping back.

His eyebrows shot up. "Who said that?"

She shrugged a shoulder innocently, enjoying his surprise. "One of Adam's staff members at the photo shoot. She also said the girls in Adam's office have a crush on you."

"Really?" he asked, grinning.

She smacked him on the shoulder. "Yes, really. She also said that you could charm the pants off anyone if you tried."

His gaze slowly made its way from her face to her toes. "Lucky you're wearing a dress, then."

"Somehow," she said, her breath coming a little faster, "I don't think choice of clothing would affect your success."

The green of his eyes grew dark, became full of promise. "There's only one thing that's stopping me from trying right now."

She swallowed. "Our personal shopper?"

"No, she's easy to deal with." His fingertips toyed with the neckline of her dress, sending sparks through her bloodstream.

"Oh." And here she'd thought the chaperone was protecting them. "Then what is it?"

He moved closer, surrounding her with his body heat. "We made a decision. In my kitchen."

"We did." She moistened her lips, and he watched the action as he spoke.

"And nothing has changed in the factors that led us to make that decision." His head dipped to kiss a spot just below her earlobe.

It took several heartbeats for her to remember what they were talking about, since his lips were working magic, drawing her into a haze of desire. "They haven't," she agreed, reaching her arms around his neck.

He kissed one corner of her mouth, then the other, his lips brushing hers, featherlight, in between. "So I won't be trying to charm your pants—or dress—off you. I won't be trying anything."

When his lips brushed past hers again, she opened her mouth, intoxicated by him, and he took the invitation, kissing her once, twice.

"Then why are you kissing me?" she asked, using the last brain cell left working in her head.

He pulled away and looked at her with heavy-lidded eyes. "That's a very good question. One I don't have a logical answer for."

She already missed his touch even though his mouth was only inches away. "Do you have an illogical answer?"

"Several," he said with a smile that melted her insides. "Starting with how you look in that dress."

"You don't look so bad yourself." He wore a lavender shirt and a silver tie that Julie had matched with it. "Speaking of our clothes, where is our personal shopper?"

"She slipped out of the room right about when I started touching the sleeve of this dress."

Faith blinked. "She's been gone all this time? She must be getting bored."

"I'll pay her a bonus for her discretion—it will be worth it." He leaned in and placed a kiss on the curve of Faith's jaw. "It's been a long, difficult month."

It had been a difficult month for him, too? "I thought that was just me."

"Why would you think that?" he asked, his voice low.

How far into her mind was she willing to let him see? She sucked her bottom lip between her teeth. There probably wasn't a point in holding back now. "You seemed so together when you came to my apartment, while I was falling apart from wanting you."

His eyebrows lifted. "I thought the same about you. You seemed unaffected, and I was having trouble keeping my hands to myself. In fact, I was getting annoyed that you were so calm."

"Not even close." She smoothed her hands over the lapels of his jacket. "In fact, I thought you must have moved on."

He let out a wry laugh. "I haven't even been able to contemplate another woman since that first night at the Santa Monica store, when you pretty much ambushed me so I would watch you work."

For a long moment she considered just staying here in

this little world they'd created. It would be like heaven. Well, until it was ripped away. Places she wanted to be were always ripped away in the end. And the longer she let herself become used to this, the worse it would hurt when it was over.

"It's been the same for me," she said. "But we've already discussed this, and standing here, so close, isn't helping any."

He drew in a sharp breath and moved back. "You're right." He scrubbed a hand through his hair and didn't meet her eyes as he said, "I'll find Julie."

# Nine

The night of the launch, Faith was a jumble of excitement and nerves as she sat beside Dylan in the back of the limousine. Going on a date with this man felt like standing at the edge of a cliff and hoping she didn't fall.

He glanced over and squeezed her hand. "Did I say you look beautiful?"

"Twice," she said, smiling. "But I don't mind."

The limo driver pulled over a short distance from the hotel. "Apparently I need to drop you here so you can walk the red carpet," he said over his shoulder.

Faith turned to Dylan. "Red carpet?"

Dylan grinned. "After the success of the Midnight Lily launch, and since Jenna has come out as Princess Jensine, we were able to attract a few more celebrities this time."

A thought suddenly occurred to her. "Will it be a

problem if you're seen on the red carpet with an employee?"

"Not in the least." He stroked his thumb over the back of her hand. "It's perfectly natural that I'd escort the florist who made the arrangements for tonight."

Put that way, it seemed reasonable, so she let out a breath and smiled.

The driver opened their door and Faith stepped out, taking in the scene around her. Paparazzi lined the street and a crowd had gathered, hoping to catch a glimpse of someone famous. The atmosphere was like nothing she'd ever experienced before and was a little intimidating.

Then Dylan was at her elbow, with a warm hand on the small of her back, grounding her. Keeping her centered.

"I don't know how Jenna lives like this," she whispered.

"Most of the time, she doesn't," he said. "She spends the majority of her days with Meg, Bonnie and Liam."

The image of a little family rose in Faith's mind—the stability, the love. Only in her mind, it wasn't Jenna's family. It was Dylan surrounded by a bunch of kids with her curly red hair and his green eyes. The image was so perfect, so unattainable, her chest ached.

"Dylan," a voice called once they reached the carpet. "Can we get a quote?"

Dylan smiled and waved, then leaned to Faith's ear. "Ebony is from a local morning show. They sometimes do a gardening segment, and I've been talking to them about doing something with us, so I need to talk to her. Can you—?" He paused, then grabbed an arm a few feet away. "Adam, I need to do a bit of media. Can you walk in with Faith? You're here alone, aren't you?"

Adam offered Faith a smile before nodding to his brother. "Sure."

He put a hand under her elbow and they walked through the door, making small talk about the weather. Once inside, he dropped her arm and asked, "Can I talk to you privately about something?"

She resisted taking a step back as his expression changed. There was something serious on his mind. Something he wasn't happy about. But he was the CEO of Hawke's Blooms Enterprises, which covered the farm, the stores, the markets and R&D, above even Dylan, so she said, "Of course," and smiled politely.

He glanced around and then led her through a door marked Staff Only into what appeared to be an office.

Then he turned and faced her squarely, face stony. "I need to ask. What do you want out of this involvement with my brother?"

Her blood turned cold at the implication about her morals. Then she crossed her arms under her breasts and matched his stance.

"What does a woman normally want out of an involvement with a man?" she asked, heavy on the sarcasm.

Without missing a beat, he began to make a list, raising a finger for each item. "Money, promotion, prestige, access to something, an opportunity to sue or blackmail. I could go on."

She coughed out a laugh, more amazed than insulted by his cynicism. "Please don't."

"If you're planning to use whatever it is between you and my brother to get ahead, it won't end well for you."

She cocked her head to the side, examining Adam's face. It was amazing how similar he looked to Dylan, yet how little they were alike. She'd seen a range of expressions on Dylan's face before but nothing this hard, this remote. Adam's green eyes were the cold arctic sea, whereas Dylan's sparked with life and energy. There was no doubt in her mind that Dylan was the better man, and she wasn't going to let his brother push her around.

She narrowed her eyes and poked her index finger into his chest. "Are you always this suspicious of people's motives?"

He looked a little less certain. "I've found it pays to be."

"Well, let me put your mind at rest." She took a step back and folded her arms again. "Hawke's Blooms has been good to me. I would never do anything to hurt the company. And Dylan? He's a good man. I would never hurt him, and anyone who wanted to would have to go through me to do it."

Adam frowned, apparently taken by surprise by her answer. "So you are planning on a future with him?"

"Actually, I'm not. But here's a question for you. How much of this—" she waved a finger, taking in the room he'd corralled her in "—is about the company and how much is about protecting your little brother?"

Adam opened his mouth to answer but then hesitated, frowned and closed his mouth again. Before he was able to find any words, Dylan burst through the door.

"What the *hell* is going on here?" His voice was tightly controlled but his gaze was clearly full of irritation aimed at his brother.

"I was just—" Adam began, but Faith had had enough and stepped in front of him.

"Your brother was grilling me about my intentions. Turns out he was worried I'd sue the company. Or was it blackmail that you were more concerned about?" she asked, moving to stand beside Dylan and smiling brightly at Adam.

Dylan's face turned red. "You said *what* to her?"

Adam held his hands up in surrender as Dylan took a step forward. "It was a reasonable concern."

"Adam, I'm warning you, get out of this room." Dylan planted his feet shoulder width apart and glared at his brother. "Now."

Adam's eyebrows shot up. "Okay, sure," he said and headed for the door. "Look, I'm sorry—"

"Not the time," Dylan said, his voice tight and fists clenching at his sides.

"Right then." Adam disappeared completely from view.

Dylan kicked the door shut behind him and then turned to Faith and blew out a breath. "I can't believe he did that. Sorry doesn't seem enough."

He seemed so tense that she laid a hand on his arm, wanting to reassure him. "No harm done. I was handling it."

One corner of his mouth quirked up. "Actually, when I opened the door, the expression on his face did seem a bit lost."

"Good," she said, satisfied she'd been able to hold her own. "You know, I think he was more worried about us as your brother than he was as the CEO."

A frown line appeared across his forehead. "What do you mean?"

"He's protective of you." Heat radiated through Dylan's

suit coat to her hand, and she rubbed his upper arm, always wanting a little more when she was near him.

He let out an exasperated breath. "He should be more worried about himself."

"Why?" The dynamics between Dylan and his brothers were endlessly fascinating to her, but then again, anything about Dylan fascinated her.

"I can't remember the last time I saw him in a relationship. Or with a woman who made him happy. I don't know why he thinks he's in any position to sort out anyone else's love life."

Her throat was suddenly tight, and she had to swallow before she could get her voice to work. "We don't have a love life. We've put a lot of effort into ensuring that."

"That's true," he said, his eyes pained. "I still love this dress on you, by the way."

She looked down at the shimmering green dress. "Thank you again. It's a lovely present." Then, unable to help herself, she looked back at him, taking in the lavender shirt and silver tie. "And I like you in that suit."

His eyes darkened. "Someone with great flair picked it out for me."

She ran a hand down the front of the shirt, remembering what it felt like to touch him without fabric between them. Without reserve.

He sucked in a sharp breath. "If we're going to leave this room, we'd better go now."

She dropped her hand and took a step back. "I think you're right."

He opened the door and gestured for her to go past, and they walked into the ballroom as if nothing had happened.

* * *

Dylan looked out over the crowd of the fashionable and famous mingling and drinking champagne in honor of Hawke's Blooms. He was still annoyed at his brother but was trying not to let it affect him. He just wanted Faith to have one perfect night to remember, and he wouldn't let Adam ruin it.

She'd bought three dates at the auction—she'd spent the first making flower arrangements at the Santa Monica store and the second making flower arrangements at Liam's research facility. Was it too much to ask that he be able to give her one night when she wasn't working, without his stupid brother ruining it?

He glanced down at Faith and pulled her a little closer against his side as they made their way through the ballroom. They were stopped by several people he knew in the industry, and he introduced Faith each time as the florist who had created the designs that adorned the room. The guests were full of praise, and although Faith didn't say it, he could feel her pride in her work. He smiled inside, knowing he'd become attuned to her feelings.

"Thank you," she whispered just below his ear once they'd moved on from another person who'd been impressed by her work.

He took a moment to appreciate the warmth of her breath on his neck before asking, "For what?"

"I told you once that my dream was to create arrangements that reached lots of people. To spread joy on that larger scale." She moistened her lips. "You've made it happen."

His chest expanded at the expression in her eyes, but he couldn't take the credit. "No, you've made it happen. I might have arranged the opportunity for Jenna, Liam and Adam to see your ideas for the Ruby Iris, but you're the one who impressed them."

"As you said, you arranged the opportunity," she said, clearly unwilling to let it drop.

"Ah, but you were creative enough in your approach to attend the auction and get my attention in the first place." He smiled down into her eyes. "You're one of a kind, Faith."

His mother appeared at his elbow, wineglass in hand. "Here you are, Dylan. I've been looking everywhere for you."

He leaned down and kissed her cheek. "Did you need something?"

"Just to check on you. Adam said something cryptic about wanting me to make sure you're all right. What happened?"

Dylan smiled tightly, not wanting to get into it with his mother. "Just big brother pushing too far."

"Don't be hard on him," his mother said indulgently. "His heart is always in the right place."

Dylan didn't say anything, letting his silence speak for him.

"Okay," his mother said, chuckling. "Sometimes he does take things too far. Now, introduce me to Faith. I've heard such good things about your work from Jenna."

Obediently, he glanced back down at his date. "Faith, this is my mother. Mom, this is Faith Crawford."

Faith smiled and held out her hand. "Lovely to meet you, Mrs. Hawke."

"You, too, Faith. But call me Andrea." She shook her

hand. "The floral arrangements are gorgeous. You've worked miracles with them."

The two women looked over at the closest arrangement, and Faith smiled. "Thank you. I made these final versions this morning out at Liam's facility, so this is the first time I've seen them under the ballroom lights."

The crystals interspersed among the blooms caught the sparkling light and refracted it into little sunbeams across the ceiling. All the guests were commenting on the effect.

"Oh, I meant to say—" Dylan's mother turned to him "—Jenna was looking for you. She wanted you to meet a journalist before you go up on stage. You go and find her and I'll keep Faith company."

Dylan looked from one woman to the other, uncomfortable about leaving them together but not completely sure why. He looked down at Faith and she patted his arm. "Go. I'll be fine."

He released her elbow and threaded his way through the crowd, restricting himself to only one last look back over his shoulder.

Faith watched Dylan walk away with the same wrench in her chest that she always felt when he left.

Women stopped him constantly, sometimes with a hand on his forearm, sometimes by putting themselves in his path. Even from a distance, she could tell he was charming them and then moving on.

"He's good with people," his mother said from beside her. "They like him."

"Yes," Faith said, turning back to face Andrea with a polite smile. "They do."

"Interesting thing is, his brothers are easier to read

than he is. It might look as if Dylan is more open than them, but he manages to keep more of himself hidden. He wears a mask of openness, which tricks people, if that makes sense."

Faith thought about conversations they'd had and the hidden depths he'd revealed. "It does make sense."

"Although he seems different with you," Andrea said casually, and then took a sip of her wine.

Butterflies leapt to life in Faith's belly. First Adam and now their mother—what was it with Dylan's family fishing for information? "You only saw us together for about ten seconds," she said, matching the other woman's casual tone.

Andrea waved the objection away with a flick of her wrist. "A mother can read between the lines. Also, I know my son, and his face is different when he speaks about you."

"He speaks about me?" Faith asked before she could think better of it.

Andrea grinned. "He's mentioned you a few times when giving me an update on this launch and your work with the Ruby Iris."

Faith could see the expectation in the other woman's eyes, the excitement that her son had found someone to settle down with. But it wouldn't be her, and that hurt more than she could let on.

She took a breath and chose her words carefully to ensure there was no misunderstanding. "I feel I need to tell you that nothing is going to happen between Dylan and me."

"Huh, that's funny. I seem to remember hearing the same story from Liam and Jenna a while ago." Her expression said Andrea wasn't deterred in the slightest. "Is this because you work for him?"

"Yes, partly. But it's more than that." Would a woman with a loving, close family even understand Faith's issues with love if she told her? Regardless, this was Dylan's mother, and it was up to him to share the parts of his life with her that he wanted.

"I'll leave it alone, then." Andrea looked up at the stage, where the tech guys were switching on microphones and getting ready. "I think the speeches are about to start."

Faith turned so that she could see the stage, her eyes easily finding Dylan in the group. He glanced up and caught her watching him, a slow smile spreading across his face. Then Jenna tapped him on the shoulder and he turned away.

"Nope," Andrea whispered. "Nothing going on between you two at all."

Faith bit down on her lip to stop the smile and watched the stage. Jenna began by welcoming everyone and gave the crowd a short history of the new flower. When she was done, Liam took the microphone and spoke of his vision in creating the Ruby Iris. Then he handed the microphone to Dylan.

Faith drank him in as he stood tall and confident at the center of the stage, but with that mask of openness, which made it seem he was sharing something with the people gathered. He was a natural, and even before he spoke, the audience was responding to him.

"Hi, everyone," he said, giving them his charmer smile. "I'm Dylan Hawke and I'd like to say a few words on behalf of the Hawke's Blooms stores. We're looking forward to working with this new flower—we think our customers will be excited to have it in their bouquets, and I know our florists are keen to create arrangements that people will love."

He walked a few steps along the stage, ensuring he was including the entire audience in his gaze. "I'd like to thank everyone who's played a part in bringing the Ruby Iris to this point, but I'd especially like to thank one of our florists, Faith Crawford, for working behind the scenes and creating these stunning arrangements we have in the room tonight. Faith, can you come up here for a moment?"

He shielded his eyes from the spotlight with the hand that still held the microphone, then raised his other hand in her direction as a round of applause flowed through the room.

Faith's pulse jumped. She hadn't expected this, but she was touched that he'd think to mention her. His mother gave her a little prod, and Faith began making her way through the crowd until she reached the two steps that led up to the small stage. Dylan reached out to steady her and moved to the side to join in the clapping.

Faith looked out over the crowd and, although the majority of people were strangers, they were smiling at her with approval. They liked her work. She'd achieved another step in her career plan—she'd reached a large group of people with her designs. She'd made them smile. She caught Dylan's gaze and mouthed, "Thank you." He nodded, his eyes sparkling.

Giving Faith's arm a little squeeze on the way past, Jenna took the microphone from Dylan and wound up the proceedings. As the music started again and the people on the stage descended to the ballroom floor, Faith was still on cloud nine. So when Dylan said, "Dance with me," she didn't hesitate.

He took her hand and led her out onto the small dance floor, where a few couples were moving to the music, and then pulled her into his arms. The clean scent of him surrounded her, and she wanted nothing more than to lean into him, to lose herself in his heat. Would she ever be able to be near him and react as if he was any other man? Or would he always have this power over her?

She needed to get her mind onto a normal topic of conversation. She cast around for an idea, then remembered that Jenna had wanted him to talk to someone earlier. "How did it go with the journalist?"

"He was from the same morning show as the woman outside. I've made an appointment to see them both tomorrow, so cross your fingers for me."

"I will." Though she was sure he wouldn't need it. Everything Dylan touched turned to gold. Except her—when he touched her, she turned to flames.

His hand on her back traced a path up, then down, leaving a trail of tingles in its wake. Faith hesitated. "Should we be doing this?"

"It's a date—our last one—and people dance on dates." He pulled her a couple of inches closer. "Besides, there are hundreds of people here. We're in no danger."

"It feels dangerous." Which was possibly the understatement of the night.

"I'll admit that it's lucky I have that limo waiting outside to take you home." His Adam's apple slowly bobbed up and down. "I don't think I could kiss you on your cheek at the door and leave tonight."

She couldn't imagine letting him walk away from her

door tonight, either. In fact, she was starting to think she would have just as much trouble leaving him here and getting into the limo.

"Speaking of the limo," she paused, moistening her lips, "I'm thinking it's probably time I went home."

"Now?" he said, coming to a standstill in the middle of the dance floor. "We haven't been here that long."

In some ways, any amount of time on this date was always going to be too long, especially now when they were touching again.

She drew in a breath, pretending this wasn't going to wrench her in two. "I was here for the speeches, I saw my arrangements in the ballroom full of people and I've danced with the most eligible bachelor in the room. What more could the night possibly bring?"

He grinned and his eyes sparkled with promise. "More dancing with that eligible bachelor."

"Yeah, that's what I'm worried about."

He chuckled. "Fair call."

The music segued from one song to another, which seemed like a natural place to end things. She stepped back, away from the circle of his arms. "Thank you for tonight. You've made it magical."

"You brought the magic," he said, his voice low.

It was too much. Being this close to him, knowing she couldn't have him, was too much. She couldn't breathe. She turned and wove her way through the crowd until she reached the door and could fill her lungs again. Dylan followed and spoke to the doorman. Within moments, the limo had pulled up in front of the door, and with a last chaste but lingering kiss on his cheek, she slipped into the backseat and left the launch—left him—behind.

# Ten

Faith sat bolt upright on the studio sofa, waiting for *The Morning Show* to start again after the ad break. Her palms were sweaty—a combination of the hot lights and a case of nerves that just might kill her—so she tried to wipe them discreetly on her skirt.

"Hey," Dylan said beside her. "Are you all right?"

"Well, I've forgotten my name. Will that be a problem?"

He chuckled and rubbed a hand up and down on her back. "They have your name written on the autocue for the host, so that doesn't matter. Just tell me you remember how to arrange flowers."

"I can do that in my sleep." Then she winced as she imagined herself fumbling. "Well, as long as I don't drop the flowers with my sweaty hands."

A man wearing a microphone headpiece waved an arm. "And we're back in three…two…one…"

The host, Lee Cassidy, a woman in her early thirties with black hair pulled tightly back from her face, scooted back into the seat at the last moment and smiled at the camera. "We have a treat for you now. Dylan Hawke, one of the brothers behind the Hawke's Blooms, and head of their hugely successful chain of florist stores, is here in the studio to tell us about a brand-new flower they launched a couple of days ago, the Ruby Iris. And he's brought along one of his florists, Faith Crawford." The host turned to them and smiled her megawatt smile again. "Welcome to the show. How are you both this morning?"

Dylan looked at Faith, giving her the chance to speak first. She opened her mouth to reply but no words came out. She closed her mouth, swallowed and tried again. Nothing. Prickles crawled across her skin.

Dylan smoothly picked up the ball. "We're both great, thanks, Lee. In fact, we're still buzzing after the launch of the Ruby Iris on the weekend. It was quite a night."

"It sounds as if it was fabulous." The host turned to the camera, giving her viewers the full benefit of her smile. "In fact, we have some photos."

The big screen behind them suddenly flashed with images from the night, including one of Faith taking Dylan's hand as she stepped up onto the stage. She was gazing up at him with her heart in her eyes. Would anyone else recognize that? Would Dylan be able to read that expression?

"So, Faith," Lee said, "tell me why you love the Ruby Iris so much. What's special about this new flower?"

Faith steeled herself. She had to answer this time.

She needed words. Any words would do. "Well, Lee, it's red."

Lee raised her eyebrows as if to say, *Is that really what you want to go with?*

Dylan leaned forward. "Of course, there are many red flowers, but there haven't been any red irises before now." He nodded at Faith, encouraging her to pick up the thought and run with it.

"That's true," she said, aware she was probably speaking too fast, but at least her vocal cords were working now. "The most popular iris has been the traditional purple, and a customer favorite is the white, and there has been pink—"

"Okay," Lee said cutting her off, "how about you show us more about this flower. We have a few things over here waiting for you."

"I'd love to," Faith said, relieved she could finally do something she was comfortable with instead of mindlessly listing flower colors.

The guy with the microphone headpiece waved at her to stand and pointed to the counter he'd shown her earlier. Lee followed him over, and the cameras panned to track their progress.

Faith stood behind a gleaming white counter with all the flowers and tools they'd brought along with them neatly laid out, and sent up a silent prayer that she didn't mess this up. Hawke's Blooms was counting on her. Dylan was counting on her.

Lee was at her side. "What are you going to make for us today?"

Faith's nerves were rising, threatening to take over; she tried to breathe through it, but it wasn't working. Then Dylan appeared at her other elbow and passed her a single white carnation. Faith took the flower, and the moment it was in her hand, she relaxed. She could do this.

As she trimmed the base of the stalk, she smiled at Lee. "I'm doing a simple arrangement that anyone at home could try. I'm going to use the Ruby Iris, but you can substitute your favorite flower—say, daffodils or tulips."

For the next few minutes, she worked on the arrangement, bringing the vision in her mind to life, giving a couple of easy jobs to Lee to do so the segment was more interesting.

When Faith was done, Lee called Dylan back into the shot and thanked them both for coming in. Then the guy with the headphones told them they were on an ad break. Lee rushed back to the sofa to be ready for the next segment, a girl with a ponytail guided Dylan and Faith off the set and within minutes, they were in Dylan's car.

Faith blinked. It was over. She'd made her first-ever TV appearance and it had consisted of her freezing and generally messing it up. Her head was still spinning.

"I'm so sorry, Dylan," she said as he slid into the driver's seat.

He started the car and glanced over at her. "What for?"

"You worked so hard to get that segment and I ruined it."

"You were great," he said cheerfully as he leaned over and squeezed her knee. She'd never met someone as skilled at manipulating the truth. If she hadn't been in the studio herself to see the train wreck, she might have believed him.

She raised an eyebrow at him and he grinned. "Okay, so you stumbled a couple of times, but your demonstration was great. You were professional, yet you explained things in ways the viewers would understand, and your love for your work shone through."

"I've let Hawke's Blooms down," she said, trying not to grimace as she said it. She didn't want pity. She wanted to apologize. "Let you down."

"Hey, you did us proud." Before he could say anything else, his cell phone rang in its cradle on the dashboard and he thumbed the Talk button. "Dylan Hawke."

"Dylan, it's Ben Matthews from *The Morning Show.* Thanks again for coming on today."

"Thank you for inviting us." Dylan pulled out to overtake a car without missing a beat in the conversation. "Anytime you want someone from Hawke's Blooms back, let us know."

"I was hoping you'd feel that way. I've just been talking to a producer from our network office in San Diego. I'd asked them to watch out for your segment today and they were impressed."

"That's good to hear," Dylan said, sliding Faith a grin.

"They've been considering a weekly gardening segment, but now they're interested in making it about flowers instead. Maybe how to arrange them, keeping them alive longer, that sort of stuff. What would you think about Hawke's Blooms doing that segment? If it goes well, we could talk about other guest spots on our LA show then."

Dylan squeezed the steering wheel harder, but his voice remained easygoing. "We'd be very interested in doing that, Ben."

"There's only one condition they've laid down. You need to have that woman from today's segment as the florist. Our social media went crazy for her when she was on air."

Faith gasped and then covered her mouth with her hand in case Ben could hear her in the background. The producers had liked her enough to make her involvement a condition? It was surreal. And people watching had liked her enough to comment about her?

"I'll talk to her and let you know," Dylan said.

"Well, talk quickly. They want you down there for tomorrow's show. You'll need to be in the studio by five a.m."

"I'll get back to you within the hour." Dylan ended the call and threw Faith a grin. "I guess you didn't ruin it."

"They want me," she said, the awe she felt coming out in her voice.

He laughed. "They sure do. What do you think? Interested?"

"Absolutely." This was the biggest thing ever to happen in her career—in her *life*—and nothing could make her let the opportunity pass.

"Then we'd better start making plans." He turned into her street. "I'll ring Ben Matthews back and work out the details. I'll also have my personal assistant book us flights and rooms in San Diego for tonight. We'll catch a late flight down and one back after the show in the morning."

His voice had been so calm, planning the details it would take to get them there, that at first she missed the significance of what he'd said. Then it hit her.

"A hotel?" she said as she wrapped one arm around herself. "Us?"

Gaze still on the road, he nodded. "They want us on set at five a.m., and I don't want to take any chances on delays. It would be much better if we're already in town."

"But we agreed…" She let her words trail off, wondering if she was making too big a deal out of this since he didn't seem worried at all.

"Don't worry about it," he said, his voice a notch lower than it had been only a minute earlier. "I'll get rooms on different floors. We'll be fine."

Okay, that seemed reasonable. Different floors should be enough distance if they were both on their best behavior.

He pulled up in front of her house. "You pack a bag and I'll let you know the time of the flight."

"Sure," she said and climbed out. As he drove away, she sighed and hoped she could trust herself to be on her best behavior if Dylan Hawke was sleeping in the same building.

The flight to San Diego was uneventful, and as soon as they arrived at the hotel, Faith excused herself to her room. She told Dylan she needed some quiet time so that her head was together for the show tomorrow, and that she'd order room service for dinner and read the book she'd brought.

But it wasn't that she needed quiet so much as a break from the tension of being with Dylan. Or, more precisely, being with him and not touching him as her body was screaming out to do. That particular tension was going to drive her insane.

And going insane just before going on live TV representing Hawke's Blooms would not help anyone. She tried to drag in a full breath but it felt as if there was an iron band around her ribs, stopping her lungs from expanding. It might have been okay to mess up last time, but tomorrow had higher stakes. It was the first of what could become a regular segment. The expectations would be higher. The crew would be anticipating someone professional. Could she be that professional?

Her cell rang, and the sudden buzzing made her jump. She checked the screen and Dylan's name flashed up. She took a breath and thumbed the Talk button. "Hey, what's up?"

"Just wanted to make sure you're okay."

Even over the phone, his voice had the power to send a shiver down her spine. "I'm fine. I've stayed in hotels before."

"About tomorrow," he said, and she could hear the smile in his voice. "You freaked out a little bit last time."

She sank down to the edge of the bed. "I'm older and wiser now."

His voice dipped, became serious. "Honestly."

"Okay." She blew out a breath. "I'm probably not wiser. Though I'm not freaking out."

"Promise?"

She lay back over the hotel bed and covered her eyes with the inside of her arm. "Maybe freaking out just a little bit. But nothing to worry about. I'll have it under control in a moment."

"Try and minimize it in your mind," he said, his voice like warm honey. "It's no big deal."

She snorted. "It's probably not a big deal for you.

You've spoken in public heaps of times. This is still big and intimidating for me."

"If you worry about it all night, you'll have yourself in a state by morning."

"Is it too late to cancel?" she asked, only half joking. "Or fly someone else up here?"

"You're the one they want."

There was something in the way he said the words that made her think he wasn't just talking about the TV spot or about business. It was in the way he said *want*, as if he was on this bed beside her, whispering the word in her ear. Her pulse picked up speed. Part of her was longing to whisper it back. Longing to walk the corridor and stairs to his room and whisper it in person. But they'd made a decision, and she needed to be strong. She pulled herself up to sit against the headboard, piling the pillows behind her, trying to focus back on the real reason for this conversation. Having her eyes closed when talking to Dylan Hawke was probably not the best way to stay focused on work.

"But if I ruin this, it's Hawke's Blooms that will suffer," she said, shifting her weight against the pillows, unable to get comfortable.

"You won't ruin it. I have every faith in you."

He meant it, too. She could tell. What she wouldn't give to have him here beside her right now, sharing his strength, his self-assurance. She always felt more anchored when he was near. Unfortunately, having him near would also kick her libido into action. What she needed was to stay on topic.

"You said yourself I'll have myself in a state by the morning. Maybe I'm not cut out for this. I'd be better off standing behind the counter back in Santa Monica."

"Think about something else." His voice was cajoling, like the devil inviting her to sin. "Go to your happy place."

"My happy place?" she asked warily.

"A memory or thought that always makes you happy. Do you have one of those that you can use?"

Her breath caught high in her throat. *Him.* "Yeah, I can think of something."

"What is it?"

"It doesn't matter," she said, attempting to sound breezy. "I've got one."

"If you tell me, I can talk you through it. Work with me here. I'm trying to help."

"Okay, it's…um…the flower markets."

"The flower markets?" he asked, skepticism heavy in his voice.

Seemed she wasn't as good at manipulating the truth as he was. Maybe more detail would help. "In the mornings, like at about two or three a.m., when they first open."

"Faith, I don't doubt you like the flower markets. But that's not the happy place you decided to use."

"Sure it is."

"Faith," he said, his voice low. "What is your happy place, really?"

"I can't tell you." She hoped that would be enough to make him drop the subject but had a sinking feeling nothing would make him do that now.

"Why?" It was a simple question, merely a word, but when it was him asking, it became more potent, and she lost her will to resist.

"Because it's you," she said on an anguished breath. "You're my happy place."

A groan came down the line. "Hell."

There was a knock on the door, and she wasn't sure if the interruption was good timing or bad. "Hang on, someone's at the door."

"I know," he said, and as she opened the door, she saw him leaning in the doorway as if he'd been there a while, his cell still at his ear, his eyes blazing.

"You're here," she said. She'd never wanted him more than in that moment. She disconnected the call and threw her cell in the direction of a table, but she missed and it fell to the floor. She left it.

Instead of answering, he reached out with his free arm and dragged her to him, his mouth landing on hers with a comfortable thud. Or maybe that sound was his cell phone dropping to the floor. He stepped forward, so she stepped backward, and he kicked the door behind them closed, blotting out all sound except breathing and the rub of fabric on fabric as they moved.

She grabbed the front of his sweater and pulled him to the bed. The pillows were still bunched in a pile at the headboard, so she maneuvered him to lie diagonally across the crisp white cover. Then she followed, not worrying about grace and finesse, just needing to touch him, to be as close to him as she could.

His leg wrapped around hers, pulling her against him, and she almost melted, but she didn't stop her frantic touching, exploring wherever she could reach. It was as if a fire burned deep inside every cell, and the only thing that could relieve the burn was Dylan. Her fingertips brushed over his jaw, his throat, needing to feel the stubble of his evening beard as if the roughness held the secrets of the universe.

As they moved, his fingers worked at her buttons

until the sides of her top fell apart. She shrugged out of it without missing a beat and was rewarded when his large palm covered a breast. She was rendered motionless, absorbing the sensations, the heat, the pure beauty of the moment.

"Dylan," she said without even realizing she was speaking.

He pulled her bra aside and leaned down, covering the peak of her breast with his mouth, using his tongue, his teeth, to make her writhe.

When he began to undo the button and zipper on her trousers, she lifted her hips, glad he was the one doing it, because operating a simple zipper was probably beyond her. Once the trousers were off, she relaxed her hips, but his hand smoothed over the front of her and her hips bucked straight back up again.

"I've been dreaming of touching you again," he said, his voice urgent. His fingers caressed her over the thin fabric, then moved underneath. At the first contact with her skin, an electric current shot through her body and she shivered.

"I've been dreaming of it, too." Fantasizing, hoping, even though she knew she shouldn't.

She tried to wriggle out of the underpants but there were hands and intertwined legs in the way, so she made no progress until he grabbed the sides and pulled them down her legs. Then he moved down her body and rested his face on her hip, his fingers toying with her, driving her crazy. His warm breath fanned over her, and the world narrowed to just this moment. She felt the weight of his head lift from her hip a moment before his mouth closed over the center of her. She gasped and moaned his name.

He moved her leg to accommodate his shoulders, and she offered no resistance—couldn't have if she'd wanted to, since every single bone in her body seemed to have dissolved. His tongue was working magic, and she was on the edge of something powerful, something glimmering in the edges of her vision. When it hit, he rode it out with her, holding her tight, his face pressed against her stomach.

Then he was gone and she heard his clothes dropping on the carpet, his belt buckle clinking as it landed, the heavy fabric of his sweater making a more muffled sound as it hit the ground. The mattress dipped as he came back into view, already sheathed, crawling over her, hovering, his features pulled taut with tension. She looped her arms around his neck and pulled him back to her, reveling in the feel of his body against hers, leg to leg, hip to hip, chest to chest.

She scraped her nails lightly across his back, eliciting a shudder, so she did it again. He reared back, lifting himself above her, and stilled. "I'm not sure I'll ever get enough of you."

A faint sense of misgiving twinged in her chest— she suspected no matter how much time she had with him, it would never be enough. She pushed the thought away. She'd take the time with him that she could get.

He began to move again, guiding himself to her, and she raised her hips to meet him. Then as he slid inside her in one smooth thrust, he held her gaze. His eyes were so dark she couldn't see the green, just an intensity she'd never known. She was trapped by it, could only move in sync with his strokes, becoming more and more lost as if pulled deeper by an exquisite undertow.

He changed his angle and the friction increased,

becoming too much, not enough. He was above her, around her, inside her. Everything was Dylan. When the fever within her peaked impossibly high, she burst free, her entire body rippling with the power of it. And while she was still flying, Dylan called her name and shuddered, joining her, holding her close.

Minutes later, she was still in his arms, trying to catch her breath. After her experience of being with this man twice now, she'd come to the realization that making love with him was nothing short of explosive.

"We did it again," she said, opening one eye to look at him.

He reached for her hand and interlaced his fingers with hers. "Perhaps it was unreasonable to stay in the same hotel and expect to keep our hands to ourselves."

She thought back over the evening, at her attempts to resist. "We almost made it."

He laughed. "We nowhere near made it. But at least you're relaxed now."

"You're right," she said and stretched. "And if I tense up in the studio, my happy place is happier than ever."

"Tense up? Then you're not relaxed enough. How about I do something about that…"

He reached for her again and, smiling, she went to him.

# Eleven

Dylan had fallen asleep, sprawled across both the bed and her, but Faith was wide awake. She wouldn't let herself fall asleep with him. She'd glimpsed heaven with him tonight, and it had made her face something.

He wasn't just her happy place. He was more than that.

She was in love with him.

Sleeping in his arms was her idea of paradise, which was why it would be emotionally reckless. How could she stay ahead of the eight ball and protect her heart if she indulged herself in sleeping beside Dylan's warm body? She couldn't let her guard down and lose her independence in whatever it was they had between them.

From the experience of her childhood, she knew she had a tendency to become attached more often and more deeply than other people did, and she'd done it again by falling in love with Dylan. He would be moving on at some point—people always did—and in the meantime the idea of coming to rely on him for anything, including letting herself fall into a routine of sleeping beside him, frightened her witless. Anytime in her past that she'd started to feel that she belonged somewhere, it had all been ripped out from under her. The path toward letting herself relax and get sucked into the belief that this could be permanent held only heartache.

She slipped out from under his arm—pausing when his breathing changed and he rolled over—and picked up her clothes. After she was dressed, she grabbed her purse and, with one last look at his sleeping form half draped by the covers, quietly slipped out of the hotel room.

She checked her watch. Ten past two a.m. The flower market would be open. She headed down to the lobby and caught a cab. Checking out the San Diego flower market had been on her list of things to do while she was here—perhaps not this early in the morning, but she was grateful for this way of keeping her mind off the man sleeping in her hotel room. The man she loved.

An hour later, she had a call on her cell from Dylan.

"Where are you?" he asked, his voice raspy from sleep but with an edge of concern.

She covered her other ear with a hand to hear better. "Down at the flower market."

"On your own?" Suddenly he sounded fully awake. "Jesus."

"I wanted to check them out."

There was scuffling on the line as if he was dragging on clothes. "Why didn't you wake me? I would have come with you."

*Because that would have defeated the purpose of finding some breathing space.* "I'm fine, and you needed the sleep."

"I'll come down there." From his tone, he was already set on his course of action.

"No need," she said quickly. "I was just about to leave." It was true anyway—she was about done, and she wanted some time back at the hotel before having to head to the studio.

"Hang tight. I'll send a car for you."

"I can catch a cab."

"The car will be there in a few minutes. I'll call you back as soon as I've ordered it, and we'll stay on the line till you're back here."

"You know," she said wryly, "this isn't my first visit to a predawn flower market."

"Indulge me."

She sighed. He wasn't going to give up, and in all honesty, it was nice that he was trying to ensure her safety. "Okay."

By the time she made it back to the hotel, Dylan was waiting in the lobby. He hauled her into his arms and held her until she could barely breathe.

"Hey," she said. "I need a little air."

He loosened his grip and led her to the bank of elevators. "Sorry. When I woke and couldn't find you… and then found you were out in the city in the middle of the night…" He punched the Up button and the doors swooshed open. Once they were inside and he'd hit the button for her floor, he gathered her against him again. "I can't remember the last time I was that scared."

She'd had no idea that he'd be so worried. That he cared that much. She rested her head against his shoulder and let him hold her. "I'm sorry. I didn't mean to worry you."

"Tell me honestly." He tilted her chin up so she met his gaze. "Why did you go down to the markets?"

It was as if she could see the universe in the depths of his green eyes, and in that moment she couldn't lie, not even to protect herself. "I needed a little space."

A bell dinged and the doors opened. Neither of them said a word until they were in her room again. Dylan headed straight for the minibar and grabbed two orange juices. He handed her one, then took a long drink from the other bottle before asking, "Space from me?"

"From us," she said, choosing her words with care. "Sometimes when I'm with you, it's intense."

He thought about that, putting his juice down and taking hers as well. Then he found her hands and interlaced their fingers. "What if we decided to give this thing between us a go? What would you think about that?"

Her pulse jumped. He cared enough to try? Although it was impossible, it meant so much that he wanted to. "We can't." She lifted one shoulder and let it drop. "The fraternization policy."

"Screw the policy," he said without hesitation.

She coughed out a laugh. "It's your company. You can't be that cavalier."

"What's the point of being one of the owners if I can't?"

"You want to change a policy that's doing some good in creating a safe workplace and protecting staff from unwanted advances, just because you want to get involved with an employee?"

"Okay, it doesn't sound good when you put it like

that. But I want to spend more time with you. I want us to be together." His eyes were solemn as he cupped the side of her face with his palm. "Is that what you want?"

Was it what she thought was in her best interests? No. What she thought would last? No. But he'd asked what she wanted. And she wanted nothing more than to be with the man she loved, so before she could stop it, a whispered "yes" slipped from between her lips.

He stepped closer and kissed her forehead tenderly. "Then we'll find a way."

Her heart squeezed tight. He sounded so determined that she didn't have the heart to say it didn't matter. She'd be moving on. Or he would be. One of them would leave; it was the way these things worked.

But maybe she could enjoy the time they had together? Just because she couldn't have forever didn't mean she couldn't have for now.

So she decided to ignore the consequences, and instead nodded and smiled and said, "I'd like that."

Five weeks later, and Faith's life was going well. Almost too well. When things fell into place this easily, it often preceded a fall, so part of her was on guard. The San Diego job was amazing—she'd become relaxed in front of the camera, and had been getting great viewer feedback on her segments. And spending more time with Dylan was her very favorite part of each day.

She was just shoving a vegetable lasagna in the oven when her cell rang. Dylan was due in about half an hour for dinner, so it was probably him letting her know he was leaving the office. Since the first trip to San Diego, they'd fallen into a pattern of spending more time together, usually at his place. They'd order takeout, maybe watch a movie, then make love, and she'd slip out and head home afterward, determined to keep her vow of not getting used to sleeping next to his warm body.

Tonight was the first time she'd agreed to have him visit her apartment. Things had been going so well, she'd let her guard slip and agreed when he'd suggested it. Her stomach was a tight ball of nerves as she wondered how she'd cope when she couldn't leave during the night. Which, of course, was probably why Dylan had suggested it...

She pulled the oven mitts off and grabbed her cell, but it was an unknown number on the screen.

"Hello?"

"Hi, is that Faith Crawford?"

Seven minutes later, Faith disconnected the call and fell onto the sofa.

She'd just been offered a job. A dream job. A nationally syndicated gardening variety show in New York had been looking for a florist to add to their team of gardeners and landscapers, and they'd seen her work on the San Diego show. Her role would be to teach people about flower arranging in a regular segment, but also to travel with a producer and record stories on high-profile floral arrangements—the ones found in the White House, in cathedrals, at big events. She'd be paid to study up close the very designs she hoped to be making one day, make contacts and share her love of flowers with a huge audience.

Yet she'd hesitated. The producer had given her a day to think about it—if she wasn't interested, they needed to know soon so they could approach someone else.

The job was full-time and in New York. She'd have to move across the country. Leave Dylan. A white-hot pain pierced her chest and she had trouble drawing a breath. Could she do it? It was unthinkable. But what if she turned the job down and stayed? When this thing with Dylan fizzled out, she'd be left without him and the dream job. And in the meantime, she'd still be working for him, so they'd have to keep sneaking around so no one guessed they were breaking company rules.

Outside, his car pulled up. She stood, tucking her hair firmly behind her ears and trying to pull herself together. What would she say to him? She'd never been more torn in her life. She might love Dylan, but her career had been her constant, the rock in her life. She *had* to take the incredible job offer in New York. To do anything less would be cheating herself and banking on a dream that could never come true.

She pulled open the front door and was confronted by the only man who'd ever touched her heart. He leaned down and kissed her and she sank into him, trying to create a memory, because she had no idea how he would react once she told him.

When they finished dinner, Faith gathered the plates and headed for the kitchen, almost as if she was escaping. Dylan followed, determined to find out what was on her mind, since she'd avoided his prodding while they ate.

"You've been distracted all through dinner," he said, standing behind her at the sink and massaging her shoulders. "Which is a shame, because that was the best vegetable lasagna I've had—and I'm not sure you even tasted it as you ate."

She turned in his arms, searching his gaze. "There's something I need to tell you."

"I'm right here." He smiled indulgently and smoothed a bright red curl back from her face.

"I had a job offer today." Her gaze didn't waver—she was watching for his reaction.

He rubbed her arms up and down, wanting to reassure her. He didn't own her. The businessman side of him hoped she'd stay at Hawke's Blooms, but the man in a relationship with her just wanted her to be happy.

"I'm not surprised. You've been doing high-profile work—one of our competitors was bound to headhunt you at some stage."

"It isn't one of your competitors," she said, sucking her bottom lip into her mouth.

He raised an eyebrow, curiosity piqued. "Who was it?"

She named the show and he let out a long whistle. "Isn't that recorded in New York?"

"The job is located there. I'd have to move."

His gut clenched as her words hit home. "What did you tell them?"

"That I'd think about it." She looked at the counter as she spoke.

He withdrew his hands and dug them into his pockets, not liking where this was headed. "And have you thought?"

She hesitated, then said, "There are so many factors to consider. I don't know what to do."

He let out a relieved breath and pulled her against his chest. "If you're not sure, then don't take it."

"Why?" she asked, her voice partly muffled by his shirt.

"I think we have something special here. Between us. If you stay, we can see where it goes." In fact, this conversation had been something of a wakeup call. He'd been happy enough going along, spending time together, making love when they could, but now that the possibility of separation had been raised, he was completely aware of how much she meant to him. He wasn't letting her go.

"Dylan," she began, but he cut her off.

"Don't decide just yet." He leaned in and placed a trail of kisses along the line of her jaw. "Give us a chance." He moved to her earlobe. He tugged it gently with his teeth and then pulled it into his mouth. She gasped and he smiled against her skin. What they had was too strong—she wouldn't leave him. And he'd never leave her.

Digging his fingers into her wild curls, he tipped her head back and claimed her mouth. Even though it had been less than twenty-four hours, it felt like forever since he'd kissed her, and he made up for the lost time. Weeks of having her in his bed at night hadn't slaked his desire for her; if anything, they had increased it. Whenever his mind wandered at work, it was always Faith it went to. The sound of her laugh, her dimples, the warmth of her mouth on him, the way her hips moved when she walked.

Her arms snaked around his waist, grabbing fistfuls of his shirt at the back, holding him in place. He loved the way she wanted him as fiercely as he wanted her.

He spun them around, away from the counter, and pressed her against the wall, kissing her, relishing the feel of her curves against him. He hooked a hand under her knee and lifted, pulling her pelvis closer, and he groaned at the delicious pressure. No woman had ever affected him this deeply or made him want this hungrily.

When her fingers worked on the buttons of his shirt, fumbling in her haste, his heart beat so hard against his ribs that she must have felt it under her hands. Finally she made it to the last button and pushed aside his cotton shirt, spreading her palms over his chest. It was as if her hands were magic; everywhere she touched she left a path of sparks, drawing him further under her spell.

Her top had a bow behind her neck, and when he pulled the end, the knot came undone. She wasn't wearing a bra, so as he peeled the front of her top down, he bared her breasts to his gaze. He cupped them with reverent hands, lifting them to meet his mouth, making her writhe against him and murmur his name. His blood heated, his pulse raced, he was helpless and she was everything.

As she undid the top button on his trousers and dipped her hand inside his pants and encircled him, he hissed out a breath between his teeth, then again as she slowly moved her hand up and down. He dropped his head to her shoulder. He was hers. No question, she owned him. After tonight, he'd make sure they were always together.

Suddenly unable to wait a moment longer, he grabbed the condom from his pocket and took off his trousers and boxers before doing the same with her underwear, not bothering to remove her skirt, just lifting it out of the way. She took the condom from him and rolled it down his length, wrapping a leg around his waist again. This time he lifted her hips, supporting her weight so that she could wrap her other leg around him as well, and then brought her down on top of him. Her sharp intake of breath mirrored his, and he paused to take in the beauty of the moment, of the sensations she evoked in his body and in his heart.

Tensing her legs, she moved up and slowly down again, and he whispered raggedly, "I love you."

The only sign that she'd heard was that her movements became faster, and he met her stroke for stroke, telling her how beautiful she was, loving the way the flesh of her bottom filled his hands. He grew more frantic, loving her, feeling the rising tension in his entire body.

He was near the edge, so close to falling over, but he held on, hovering, unwilling to go alone. He reached down between them, found her most sensitive spot and caressed until she exploded, moaning his name, contracting around him so tightly that he couldn't hold a moment longer. He let go, calling out the name of the woman he loved.

When Faith woke the next morning, she was alone. She reached out to feel the other side of her bed and found it rumpled but cold. Rising quickly, she slipped on a robe and padded through the apartment, finding no trace of Dylan.

A small part of her was relieved. She'd made a decision during the night to take the job and didn't think she could face telling him just yet. She knew that was cowardly—of course it was—but how could she face the man she loved and tell him she was leaving? Instead, when they'd made love, she'd said goodbye with her touch. In every silent way she could.

Maybe tomorrow, or once she was packed and her

flight was booked, she would drop in to see him and try to explain. Maybe by then she'd have found the words.

She pulled on some clothes and dragged the boxes she always kept on standby out of the hall closet. It wouldn't take long—being wary of putting down roots meant she liked to be ready to pick up and travel when the need struck, so packing was easy.

She was on her living room floor, surrounded by sealed and half-packed boxes, when Dylan returned. In one hand he held a takeout tray with two coffees and a pastry bag, and in the other, a bunch of flowers. But his expression…his expression was going to haunt her dreams.

Dylan froze on the threshold to Faith's apartment, feeling as if he'd been sucker punched.

When he'd woken this morning, he'd been so damn filled with love and optimism, all he could think about was waking like this every morning. Of spending the rest of his life with her. He'd slipped out without waking her to hunt down the perfect engagement ring. He knew it couldn't be a standard diamond for Faith, and he'd found a purple diamond in a platinum setting in a window and convinced the owner to open early for him.

He'd been on cloud nine, seeing a rosy future in front of them, seeing everything he'd never known he wanted all wrapped up in one gorgeous woman. Faith. Telling her he loved her last night had felt right, deep in his soul. She might not have said the words back, but he was in no doubt that she loved him. Not after the way she'd been touching him last night.

He'd hoped she'd still be asleep when he got back with breakfast and the ring, but it had taken a little lon-

ger than he'd planned. Still, the last thing he'd expected
to see was her getting ready to flee.

Again.

Especially after spending a night together that had
rocked his world. It was as if all the air in the room—in
his life—had been sucked out, leaving him in a vacuum.

"Going somewhere?" he asked mildly.

"Uh, yes."

He took a step inside but couldn't bring himself to
sit down or even cross the room. Not when she was surrounded by those damn packing boxes. "You're taking
the job, aren't you?"

"It's an incredible opportunity." Her voice was laced
with guilt, and she wouldn't meet his eyes. It seemed
that they weren't on the same page about this relationship at all.

"When did you decide?" he asked, not 100 percent
sure he wanted to know the answer. "Just now, or had
you already made up your mind last night?"

She was silent, which pretty much answered his
question. He wanted to throw up.

"So you'd made up your mind and were obviously
hoping to skip out this morning while I wasn't looking. Were you planning on ever telling me? Or perhaps
the plan was a quick call from New York after you'd
arrived?"

"I was definitely going to talk to you." She finally
looked up and met his gaze, and he could see that much
was true. Shame about the rest.

"So," he said and drew in a breath, steeling himself,
"telling you last night that I love you doesn't mean anything to you?"

"Of course it does, but love isn't enough, Dylan. It's

not steadfast." She moistened her lips, her beautiful brown eyes pained. "You have to understand that my career is the only thing I've ever been able to count on."

Suddenly Dylan was angry. She was giving up because she didn't think she could count on them? On him? He dropped the flowers on the coffee table and slid the takeout tray down beside the bouquet. Then he reached into his pocket, found the little velvet box, held it up and opened it.

"How's this for steadfast?" he said, forcing each word out past a tight jaw. "I was willing to commit my life to you."

She flinched. "I'm sorry. But you say that now—"

"I said it last night, too," he pointed out, setting a clenched fist on his hip.

She brushed at a tear as it slid down her cheek. "Thing is, I believe you. I promise I do. But once the novelty wears off, you'll be gone. It was never going to last."

"Explain that to me," he said, not caring that his exasperation was coming through in his tone. "Explain how you know what I'll do."

She collected her hair up in her hands, and then let it drop as she sat back on her heels. "One thing I've learned is that love is fickle. All my life I've seen the proof of people's attraction to the next bright, shiny thing. *I* was never enough. My aunt who loved me for a year then gave me up when she got pregnant. My mother who loved me but was always leaving for the next big adventure. My grandparents who loved me but were always relieved when someone else took me in. My father who loved me but wouldn't arrange a job on land so I could live with him. You might love me, Dylan," she said, her voice cracking on his name, "but something else will come along, snag your attention and drag you away. I will never allow myself to be in the position of thinking I'm not enough again."

He'd known she had a rough childhood and that made trust difficult for her, but he couldn't believe she thought their relationship wasn't worth fighting for. Wasn't worth giving a chance. She didn't think he was worth taking a risk on. Weariness suffused every cell in his body.

"You know, you say people leave, but you're the one leaving. It's always you leaving, either sneaking out of my place after we make love, or leaving early from the launch, or going to the flower market at two in the morning."

Then he dropped the ring on the hall stand and glanced over his shoulder. "Ever heard the phrase 'Be careful what you wish for'? You've been expecting me to leave since day one, and here I go."

He walked out the door and across the small courtyard to his car without once looking back.

# Twelve

Faith sat on a plastic chair at the window of her tiny New York apartment, chin in her hands as she looked down at the street below. She'd been here for only two weeks, so it wasn't strange that it didn't feel like home yet…though when had anyplace ever felt like home?

She loved the new job, but deep in her soul she'd been numb from the moment she'd arrived. No, before. She'd always been alone, but this loneliness was different—it was a yearning for one person. A tall, flirtatious man with sparkling green eyes and hair like polished mahogany.

Since she'd learned the hard lessons about life as a child, she'd always been emotionally self-sufficient, but something had changed. She'd developed relationships. She'd never let a person get as close to her, under her guard, as Dylan had. But it wasn't just him—she'd become friends with Jenna.

Jenna had called to congratulate her when she'd heard about the job, and they'd kept in touch since she moved. They'd spent a lot of time together while organizing the launch of the Ruby Iris, but at the time, Faith had thought of them as colleagues working together. Now she realized what Jenna had known then—they'd become friends.

Somewhere along the line, Faith had learned to believe in people again.

Desperate to hear a friendly voice, she picked up her cell and dialed Jenna's number.

Jenna picked up on the first ring, her lilting voice a little breathless. "Hi, Faith."

"Is this a bad time?" Faith asked. She was acutely aware that Jenna had two babies and her time was often not her own.

"Now is good. We're out back in the double stroller, walking along the flower beds. As long as I keep pushing them, I can talk to you until snack time."

Faith's mind drifted to when she'd worked on-site at the flower farm and could wander along those same flower beds during her lunch break, sometimes chatting with Jenna or carrying one of the babies on her hip. "Give them both a cuddle from me when you get a chance."

"Will do. How are you?"

"It's all good here." Faith smiled as she said it, hoping it would make her voice sound happy. "Just home from work and felt like a chat."

There was a pause. "Have you talked to Dylan lately?"

By an unspoken rule, they'd never spoken about Dylan, and Faith wasn't sure how much Dylan had told his sister-in-law of what had happened between them. "Um, no. I don't think we've had a chance to touch base since I arrived."

"A chance to touch base? That sounds as if you're talking about an acquaintance."

"Dylan and I worked together," she said carefully.

Jenna laughed. "You're not honestly going to try to tell me that nothing happened between you two. I haven't pushed you on it because I realize things must have been messy, but I've never seen two people who looked at each other the way you guys did. It was intense."

Faith's eyes stung with tears that she wouldn't let fall—they *had* been intense. She swallowed before she could reply. "So Dylan hasn't said anything?"

"No, which isn't like him. I can usually wheedle information out of him, but when your name comes up, he clams up. Come on," she said, her voice ultrasweet, "tell Aunty Jenna what happened. You know you want to."

Jenna was right—having no one to talk to about it had made her heart feel even heavier. "But Dylan is your family…"

"Don't worry about that. If he's treated you badly, I'll be mad at him, but he'll always be Bonnie's uncle and soon he'll be Meg's uncle too. There's nothing you can say about Dylan that will ruin my relationship with him. Tell me what he did."

"He didn't do anything," Faith admitted. "It was me." She curled her legs up underneath her on the hard chair and told Jenna the whole story.

"So," Jenna said when Faith was done, "Dylan loves you but you won't trust him to stick around?"

Already feeling raw from reliving everything that

had happened, the words hit her hard. "It's not about trusting him—it's about relationships in general. I... have trouble believing in them."

"Faith, Dylan is the most steadfast man you're ever likely to meet. He's devoted himself to his family's business since he was a child. He's always there for his brothers, for his parents, for me. You might have trouble believing in relationships, but if Dylan offers a commitment, he means it."

The floor was falling away from under her feet, and all Faith could do was squeeze her eyes shut. He'd been prepared to commit to her as well, but she'd thrown it away. Had she made the biggest mistake of her life?

A man who was committed to all the things in his life that were important to him was nothing like her own family, yet she'd been expecting him to behave the way they had. She'd taken her issues with her family out on him.

She hadn't been fair to either one of them. Her stomach clenched and dipped.

Unfortunately, even if it was a mistake, it was too late. After their last morning together, he wouldn't ever want to see her again. The pain in his eyes when he'd seen her packing her things had felt like a slap.

He would never trust her again, and she couldn't blame him.

Dylan sat in a wingback in his pristine white-on-white living room and swore. Then he took another mouthful of the beer he'd been nursing for a good ten minutes. This room was mind-numbingly dull. How had he never noticed that before? The interior designer who'd done the place had told him it would look modern, crisp and fresh. But it looked bland.

Like his entire life.

When Faith left, she'd taken all the damn sunshine with her. He hadn't found the energy to get excited about—or even interested in—anything for weeks. Maybe he never would again.

He took another swig of the beer.

Regardless, he shouldn't be giving her another thought. She'd given up on what they had, on their future. Hell, she'd left the state without a second thought. The best thing he could do was forget her. Which, naturally, was easier said than done.

There were voices at his door, and then the sound of people letting themselves in. Only his housekeeper, parents and brothers had their own keys. His parents had enough manners not to use them, and it was his housekeeper's day off. Which left his brothers. He sighed. He was in no mood to see them or anyone.

"I'm not home," he called out.

Ignoring him, Adam and Liam headed through the entryway, straight for him.

"So this is your answer," Adam said, shaking his head. "Drinking on a Saturday morning."

"I'm not *drinking*. I'm having a beer and watching football."

Liam made a point of looking around the room. "Are you doing it telepathically? Or hadn't you noticed the TV isn't on?"

"Not yet, smartass. I was about to switch it on when you barged in here. Also, I want the keys back."

Adam crossed his arms over his chest. "We're worried—this isn't like you. Tell us what you're going to do about your relationship."

Dylan looked away. "I don't have a relationship."

"With Faith," Adam said with exaggerated patience.

Dylan pointed a finger at his brother. "I seem to recall you were the one constantly telling me not to get involved with her."

"True." Adam nodded, seemingly unperturbed. "And my word should be law to my younger brothers. Yet you ignored me and went ahead anyway. What does that tell you?"

"That you're deluded about the extent of your power over us?" Dylan looked down at his beer. There was only half left. He was going to need a lot more alcohol to make it through this conversation.

Liam dropped onto a sofa across from him. "That's a good point, and we'll return to that later. But Adam's right. You broke company policy for this woman. I wouldn't have believed it if I hadn't been there watching the whole thing unfold."

"I made a mistake," Dylan said and took another swig of his beer, hoping they didn't see through him, because he'd make that same mistake again in a flash if it meant more time with Faith.

Adam blew out a breath. "I saw the way you and Faith defended each other at the launch. You're in love. Both of you. So why are you drinking here alone?"

Dylan flinched. That was a hell of a question, but not one he wanted to get into with his brothers. "She's gone. Feel free to follow her lead, and make sure you close the door on the way out."

Propping one ankle on a knee, Liam leaned back in the sofa. "Did you ask her to stay?"

*Did he ask her to stay?* What sort of idiot did they take him for? He drew in a measured breath before replying. "Of *course* I asked her to stay. I even bought her a damn ring."

Liam rubbed a hand over his jaw. "I've come to know Faith, and I think I understand her."

Adam and Dylan both turned disbelieving eyes to him.

Liam shrugged. "Okay, Jenna understands her. But still, she told me a couple of things."

Adam sighed. "If Jenna had some ideas, out with it."

"Faith didn't need a ring," Liam said, leaning forward and resting his forearms on his knees. "She needed you, you moron. Words have always come easy to you, and she knows that, so how would she know what to believe?"

Dylan frowned. "Jenna called me a moron?"

"No, that part was me. But listen up. You have to do something to *show* her that you're in it for the long haul. That you'll stand by her." Liam's eyes narrowed. "You are in it for the long haul, aren't you?"

"Would I have bought her a ring if I was going to bail out?"

Adam nodded. "So if you want her back, you won't be able to rely on your gift of gab. You can't just talk— you'll have to show her."

For a long moment, Dylan was speechless. They were right. He'd known her childhood had been full of promises that had quickly been broken—how had he not realized he'd need to do something more?

People had loved her in the past only when she fitted into their lives, and he'd pretty much asked her to say no to a new job for him. He rubbed his hand down his face. Hell, he'd asked her to give up a great opportunity because he lived in LA—to fit in with his life.

Adam dug his hands into his pockets. "Final question, then we'll leave. Is what you had with Faith worth fighting for?"

Dylan stilled. Was it too late to show her that his love didn't depend on anything else? That he'd take her on her own terms? And how would he show her? He'd have to make a change in his life *for* her. So she wouldn't simply have to fit in with him ever again.

He reached for his cell. "Let yourselves out," he said without looking at his brothers. "And leave your keys. I was serious about that."

He didn't have to look up to know his brothers were smiling, but he ignored them and made a call. He had several calls to make and was impatient to get going. The sooner he started on the plan that was forming in his mind, the sooner he could see Faith.

Excitement bubbling away in her belly, Faith checked the address again and looked up at the building. Yes, the gorgeous apartment building on the edge of Central Park was the right place.

Jenna had called a couple of days ago, saying she'd be in New York for a few days visiting a friend and would love to meet up, and Faith had jumped at the offer.

A doorman asked if he could help, and Faith said she was visiting a friend in 813. The doorman smiled and said she was expected, and then ushered her to the elevator.

Once she'd found the right floor, she buzzed the button outside apartment 813 and waited. But when the door swung open, it was Dylan on the threshold, not Jenna. He looked so tall and solid and gorgeous and *Dylan* that Faith's throat tightened too much to speak. So she just stood there and drank in the sight of him.

After what seemed like an eternity, he cleared his throat. "Come in," he said.

Still without speaking, she walked in, and he closed the door behind her. Such simple actions, but weighted with so much meaning. Expectation. Hope.

The apartment was empty of furniture, but it was beautiful—huge, filled with light, and with great views of the park through floor-to-ceiling windows. But as soon as Dylan was in front of her again, she couldn't look at the room. Or speak.

"Hi," he said eventually, his voice raspy.

"Hi," she whispered back.

Being this close again, it seemed natural, necessary even, to reach out and touch him…but she didn't have that privilege anymore. He'd offered it to her and she'd declined it. She'd left, just as he'd accused her of doing.

She dropped her gaze to the floor. "I came to see Jenna."

"I know." But he didn't make any move to summon Jenna or do anything else. The tension in the room was thick enough to press down on her, make her want to run. But she wouldn't leave this time, not when she had this chance to be near him, if even for a few minutes.

She took a breath, steeled herself and looked at him again. "How are you?"

He lifted one shoulder and then let it drop. "As well as can be expected. You?"

"Good," she said, but her voice cracked, so she added, "I'm good." Her hands trembled with the intensity of seeing him and not touching him, not being able to speak freely. Of being alone with him. "Is Jenna here?"

"No," he said simply.

Suddenly the strangeness of the situation hit her. Seeing Dylan again had fried her brain, so she hadn't put two and two together right away. "Whose apartment is this?"

"Yours." His expression didn't change, giving nothing away.

She took a step back. "What do you mean?"

"I've had a contract for this place drawn up in your name—" he gestured to some paperwork on the kitchen counter through an archway "—but if you'd rather have a different apartment, we can tear this contract up and keep looking."

"I already have a place to live," she said warily.

"It's a present. Although," he said, casting a quick glance around, "if you wanted, this place is big enough for both of us."

"Both of us?" she repeated, not daring to believe he meant what she thought he was saying.

He nodded, his beautiful green eyes not sparkling now—they were too somber. "If you'll have me. Or you can have it for yourself if you choose not to invite me back into your life. No strings attached. A parting gift. Completely your choice."

"My choice?" She circled her throat with a hand. He really wanted her back?

"Or if you don't like the city," he said with a casual shrug, despite his entire body being tense, "we could move farther out, and you can commute for your job. Whatever you want, I'll make it work."

She paused as the pieces of what he was saying

clicked together. "Hang on. You're willing to move to New York?"

"In an instant," he said without hesitation. "If that's what it takes."

It was so unexpected, she couldn't get her head around it. "What would you do here? Your company is on the West Coast."

He rubbed his fingers across his forehead. "I've been thinking that I could open some Hawke's Blooms stores on the East Coast. It makes business sense."

She checked his expression more closely and realized he was sincere. "That's quite a change in your role—moving away from managing the existing stores to starting small again."

"We can employ people to oversee the existing stores to free me up to start the new ones. I've realized that's what I love doing—the buzz and excitement of starting something new. You gave me that by pushing me to think about my own dreams." He reached out and cradled the side of her face in his palm. "Have I thanked you for that?"

She leaned into his palm and laid her hand over his, pressing in, making the contact more solid. "You just offered me an apartment, Dylan. I don't think you need to do anything else."

He took a small step closer. He was so close, she could feel his body heat. Her lungs struggled to find enough air. She released his hand from her cheek, and he let it fall to his side.

"Loving you means I like to do things for you."

"You know," she said looking up at him from under her lashes, "all of this is a big risk for you, given you don't even know if I love you back."

One corner of his mouth turned up in a cocky grin. "Are you going to deny it?"

She was immediately sorry she'd teased. She sucked in her bottom lip between her teeth, trying to think of the best thing to say. She couldn't lie, but it didn't feel like the right time to tell him that she loved him for the first time. It should be special.

His grin stretched wide. "No need to say it. I already know you love me, despite your unwillingness to admit it."

"You always were confident." She wanted to chuckle, but a thick ball of emotion had lodged in her throat and she was worried that if she tried to laugh, she'd cry instead.

He took her hands and held them between their bodies. "You can keep leaving, Faith, but as long as you love me, I'll keep following, even if I have to open stores in every damn state."

His words were the last straw—she burst into tears, and Dylan drew her against his body. Everyone in her life before had found a loophole to get rid of her. By leaving, she'd given Dylan a huge loophole—and he simply went around it to follow her. Jenna was right— he was the most steadfast man she was ever likely to meet. He was a man she could trust to stand by his word.

She pulled back so she could see his eyes, still hiccupping as the tears pressed in on her. In his gaze, she saw his love, his commitment, and she knew she could finally completely trust that he really wanted to be with her and would stay for the long haul.

"I love you, Dylan Hawke," she said, her heart full to bursting.

He lifted her off her feet and spun her around. "I can't tell you how glad I am to hear you say that."

"Hey," she said on a surprised laugh, "I thought you said you already knew."

He gently set her down and tucked her hair behind her ears. "I did, but it's still nice to hear it said aloud."

"I'll be sure to say it often, then." Her voice was barely more than a whisper.

He leaned in and kissed her. She wrapped her arms around his neck, pulling him closer. Weeks of not seeing him, not touching him, not kissing him, had built into a need that she was finally free to let loose.

When he pulled back, his breathing was heavy, but he was smiling. "Do you still have the ring I left on your hall stand in LA?"

She reached down to grab her purse where she'd dropped it, and then dug around before producing the precious little velvet box. "I've had it with me every day."

She passed it to him with an unsteady hand. When he'd left it in her apartment, she'd closed the box and hadn't opened it again, so she'd had only the one fleeting glance at the ring from across the room when he'd shown it to her in anger. She might have carried it with her ever since, but she hadn't given in and peeked inside. Technically it was still Dylan's ring, and she'd known she should give it back, but she hadn't been able to bring herself to do it.

He took the box from her, opened it and retrieved the purple diamond ring.

"More than anything in the world," he said, his voice low, "I want to be your husband and you to be my wife. Faith Crawford, will you marry me?"

"I want that so badly." She swiped at the tears still rolling freely down her cheeks. "Yes, I'll marry you."

He slid the ring onto her finger and then kissed her slowly, reverently. As he pulled away, he whispered against her mouth, "I think this is the start of our biggest adventure yet."

\* \* \* \* \*

*If you loved this Hawke Brothers novel,
read more in this series from
reader favorite Rachel Bailey*

*THE NANNY PROPOSITION
and
HIS 24-HOUR WIFE
(available October 2015)*

*Also try these other books from Rachel Bailey*

*COUNTERING HIS CLAIM
RETURN OF THE SECRET HEIR
MILLION-DOLLAR AMNESIA SCANDAL*

*Available now from Harlequin Desire*

*If you're on Twitter, tell us what you think of
Harlequin Desire! #harlequindesire!*

# COMING NEXT MONTH FROM

# ⊞ HARLEQUIN® *Desire*

## Available October 6, 2015

### #2401 A CONTRACT ENGAGEMENT • by Maya Banks
In this reader-favorite story, billionaire businessman Evan Ross has special terms for Celia Taylor, the sexy ad executive desperate to seal a career-making deal. But she's turning the tables with demands of her own...

### #2402 STRANDED WITH THE BOSS
*Billionaires and Babies* • by Elizabeth Lane
Early tragedy led billionaire Dragan to steer clear of children. But could a spunky redhead—who's suing his company!—and her twin toddlers melt his frozen heart when they're stranded together in a winter cabin?

### #2403 PURSUED
*The Diamond Tycoons* • by Tracy Wolff
Nic Durand had a one-night stand with the reporter exposing corruption in his company. Now she's having his child. She may be set on bringing him down, but he'll pursue her until he has her right where he wants her!

### #2404 A ROYAL TEMPTATION
*Dynasties: The Montoros* • by Charlene Sands
When Princess Portia Lindstrom shows up at his coronation, it's love at first sight for King Juan Carlos. But soon her family's explosive secret could force the unwavering royal to choose between his country's future and his own.

### #2405 FALLING FOR HER FAKE FIANCÉ
*The Beaumont Heirs* • by Sarah M. Anderson
Frances Beaumont needs a fortune. CEO Ethan Logan needs a Beaumont to give him credibility when he takes over the family brewery. Can this engagement of convenience lead to the real deal?

### #2406 HIS 24-HOUR WIFE
*The Hawke Brothers* • by Rachel Bailey
Their spontaneous Vegas marriage should have ended the day after it began! But when they partner on a project, Adam and Callie must pretend they're still together to avoid a high-profile scandal. Will they soon want more than a short-term solution?

---

**YOU CAN FIND MORE INFORMATION ON UPCOMING HARLEQUIN® TITLES, FREE EXCERPTS AND MORE AT WWW.HARLEQUIN.COM.**

HDCNM0915

He was the most beautiful man she'd ever seen.

Desi Maddox knew that sounded excessive, melodramatic even, but the longer she stood there staring at him, the more convinced she became.

His emerald gaze met hers over the sea of people stretching between them and her knees trembled. Her heart raced and her palms grew damp with the force of her reaction to a man she'd never seen before and more than likely would never see again.

It was a deflating thought, and exactly what she needed to remind herself of what she was doing here among the best and brightest of San Diego's high society. Scoping out hot men was definitely not what her boss was paying her for. Unfortunately.

Wanting to free up her hands, she turned to place her glass on the empty tray of yet another passing waiter. As she turned back, though, her eyes once again met dark green ones. And, this time, the man they belonged to was only a couple of feet away.

She didn't know whether to run or rejoice.

In the end, she just stared—stupefied—up into his too-gorgeous face and tried to think of something to say that wouldn't make her sound like a total moron. Her usually quick mind was a blank, filled with nothing but images of high cheekbones. Shaggy black hair that fell over his forehead. Wickedly gleaming eyes. The sensuous mouth turned up in a wide, charming smile. Broad shoulders. And height. He was so tall she was forced to look up, despite the fact that she stood close to six feet in her four-inch heels.

"You look thirsty," he said, and—of course—his voice matched the rest of him. All deep and dark and husky and wickedly amused. "I'm Nic, by the way."

"I'm Desi." She held out her hand. He took it, but instead of shaking it as she'd expected, he held it as he gently stroked his thumb across the back.

It was so soft, so intimate, so not what she'd been expecting, that for long seconds she didn't know what to do. A tiny voice inside her was whispering for her to escape from the attraction holding them in thrall. But it was drowned out by the heat, the *sizzle*, that arced between them like lightning.

"Would you like to dance, Desi?" he asked.

She should say no. But even as the thought occurred to her, even knowing that she might very well get burned before the night was over, she nodded.

*Don't miss PURSUED*
*by* New York Times *bestselling author Tracy Wolff,*
*available October 2015 wherever*
*Harlequin® Desire books and ebooks are sold.*

www.Harlequin.com

# Turn your love of reading into rewards you'll love with
# Harlequin My Rewards

**Join for FREE today at
www.HarlequinMyRewards.com**

Earn **FREE BOOKS** of your choice.

Experience **EXCLUSIVE OFFERS** and contests.

Enjoy **BOOK RECOMMENDATIONS**
selected just for you.

**PLUS!** Sign up now
and get **500** points
right away!

Earn
FREE
REWARDS
HarlequinMyRewards.com
Join
Today!

MYR16R

# THE WORLD IS BETTER WITH

*Romance*

Harlequin has everything from contemporary, passionate and heartwarming to suspenseful and inspirational stories.

Whatever your mood, we have a romance just for you!

Connect with us to find your next great read, special offers and more.

f /HarlequinBooks

🐦 @HarlequinBooks

www.HarlequinBlog.com

www.Harlequin.com/Newsletters

## ⬡ HARLEQUIN®

A *Romance* FOR EVERY MOOD™

www.Harlequin.com